T3-AOR-444

GUNFIGHT AT
FRIO CANYON

GUNFIGHT AT FRIO CANYON

•

Kent Conwell

AVALON BOOKS
NEW YORK

PRINTED IN THE UNITED STATES OF AMERICA
ON ACID-FREE PAPER
BY HADDON CRAFTSMEN, BLOOMSBURG, PENNSYLVANIA

To my son, Todd, good luck and hang in there.
And to my wife, Gayle, let's go to the beach.

Chapter One

Riding south out of Kerrville, Texas, I spent the night in Camp Verde just north of Bandera Pass. Twelve years earlier, Camp Verde had been the home of Jefferson Davis's embarrassing experiment with camels. At the end of the experiment, the camels had vanished like ghosts into the rugged desolation of West Texas, leaving behind a single mission for the Yankee bluecoats—to hold the Comanches at bay.

Having ridden with Nathan Bedford Forrest when he raided the Yankees in Tennessee in '62 and '63, I had built a mighty large distaste for the boys from the North, enough so that I was as uneasy around those bluecoats as a crib girl at Bible study. That's why I didn't hang around Camp Verde more than one night.

1

When I rode out next morning, the mistake I made was not continuing on down to Bandera. If I had, I would never have been accused of killing an old rancher and stealing his savings. And if that wasn't enough to fan the fire, I found myself neck-deep in Comanches, bushwhackers, and a mama desperate to marry off her two daughters: one who thought herself better that the Good Lord, the other a tomboy who sometimes needed a kick in the rear to get her attention.

The entire Frio Canyon episode came about because, as usual, I was where I shouldn't have been. I was sitting at a poker table, staying about even. Naturally, I was drinking Old Orchard whiskey; and naturally, I listened when I should have plugged my ears. But, when the drifter from Uvalde starting talking about the fine land around the Frio Canyon area, I perked up.

A small ranch of my own had been a lifelong dream.

Since I had no pressing meetings with rich bankers or important lawyers, I decided to mosey on down to that neck of the woods to see for myself. I had always wanted my own place. So, when the drifter swore the country was prettier than a spotted dog under a red wagon, and that the sweet water in its streams was colder than a well digger in Montana, I decided to take a look for myself.

And that's how I came to rein up on the rim of a precipitous bluff overlooking a fast-flowing river.

I slumped back in my center-fire rig and sighed. Removing my John B. Stetson, I dragged my sleeve across my forehead. "I reckon this is one skin-blistering day, Bill," I said to the gray gelding I rode, glancing up at a sun so hot that even the chickens were laying hard-boiled eggs.

My stomach growled. I'd been on short rations since Camp Verde, and my empty belly was rattling.

Down below, the river bubbled and swished along the rocky canyon floor, its water clear as crystal, and I knew it would be cold as ice. I figured that had to be the Frio. "What do you say we amble down there and make us a camp, Boy?" At that moment, two deer emerged from a tangle of berry briars downriver and lowered their heads to drink. I reached for my saddle gun. "And could be I'll have fresh meat toni—"

The words clogged in my throat. Further downriver, a small band of Indians rode out from under the pecan and oak lining either side of the river.

Quickly, I backed my pony away from the rim and dismounted. Tying him to a nearby cedar, I dropped to my belly and slithered across the rocky ground back to the rim.

I counted five, watering their ponies and splashing the clear water over their lean, muscular bodies. After a few moments, they turned in my direction. Muttering a curse under my breath, I remained motionless. I held my breath as they passed below and continued upriver.

After about half a mile, they left the river's edge and angled back under the canopy of pecan and oak, emerging on a trail leading to the rim.

I jumped to my feet and swung into the saddle. "Let's go, Bill. If they're coming up, we're going down."

Hurrying along the rim of the bluff, I discovered a slope of talus spreading to the river's edge. Pausing, I looked over my shoulder and grinned with relief when I saw that I'd put a couple bends in the canyon between them and me.

Dismounting, I led Bill down the slope, slowly picking our way over the shattered and slivered shale and limestone. When I reached the river, I turned south and rode hard.

An hour before sundown, I figured I had put five or six miles between me and the Indians, but knowing where there was one rattler there could be others, I picked a campsite back in a tumble of boulders at the base of the bluff. After tending Bill, I stacked rocks in the shape of a horseshoe in the middle of which I built a small fire, confident no one could spot the flames from even ten feet away. I put coffee on to boil, figuring the breeze whiffling every which way through the trees would cause the aroma of the coffee to dissipate. I didn't even considering bringing down a deer. Instead, I snared a fat cottontail.

Just before sundown, when the shadows began filling the canyon, I heard the distant bawling of cattle. I peered into the encroaching darkness but saw nothing.

Then I heard the click of hooves on rock. Slipping my Winchester from the boot on my saddle, I eased from the shelter of my boulders. A lone rider was pushing five or six head of cattle downriver. Where in the blazes had he come from? Considering the Indians I'd spotted, he was a mighty lucky jasper. I considered letting him ride on by, but about the time he drew even with me, he turned in my direction and called out, "Hello. Anyone there?"

I remained silent.

He called out again, "Anyone out there?"

With a frown, I replied, "Just me."

He chuckled. "Who's me?"

I remained behind a boulder. "Just a drifter making camp."

He chuckled again. "Thought I caught a tiny whiff of Arbuckle's. A cup would taste right good."

"Come on in."

The sharp clatter of iron shoes on rocks echoed through the shadows as the rider slowly made his way to the fire. He held up his hand. "Howdy, Stranger." He wore a broad, amiable grin.

He remained in the saddle, awaiting an invitation to climb down. He wore a sidearm, but he kept his hands on the saddle horn. His eyes studied my camp. "Expecting company?"

"Ran across some Indians this afternoon. Upriver. Don't figure on taking chances."

His brows knit. "Upriver? I come down it this afternoon with these strays."

"You're a lucky gent," I replied. "I don't reckon you'd be one to get in a poker game with."

He glanced worriedly over his shoulder. "I ain't that lucky."

"You got some sense of smell."

He grinned and wiggled his button nose. "That's what my ma always said."

"Help yourself to the coffee if you got a cup. Use mine if you don't."

He dismounted smoothly and dropped the reins to the ground. "Always carry one," he said, digging in his saddlebags. He squatted by the fire and poured himself a cup. Cradling it in both hands, he sipped it and sighed. "That's mighty good coffee. Sure obliged." He pushed his hat onto the back of his head, revealing a tangle of red hair that looked like kittens had sucked on it. He looked up. "Name's FW Red, from the Bar F back south of here. Been out running down strays."

"Howdy," I replied, replenishing my own coffee. "Lew Hobbs is what they call me. And I reckon you can see I'm just a—drifting."

He glanced around into the darkness. "Ain't nothing wrong with that, Hobbs."

I knelt by the broiling rabbit. "Hungry?"

He licked his lips, and I could see the eagerness in his eyes. "I'd be obliged."

With a chuckle, I pulled off a hind leg and tossed it to him. "I got more here than I can handle."

He tore off a mouthful, and while he was chewing, said, "I can always put grub away." He took another bite and glanced into the darkness behind him. "Truth is," he said, lowering his voice, "I was mighty glad to see you. We got word that there be some rogue Comanches running loose. I wasn't none too keen on spending the night out here all by my lonesome."

"Plenty room," I said, nodding to the area surrounded by the boulders. "When you finish gnawing on that T-bone steak there, you best bring your pony in."

"You read my mind." His eyes drifted down to my waist. "You best strap on your sidearm, Hobbs, just in case."

I stared into my coffee cup. "I don't wear one."

"Huh? You mean you don't wear no six-gun?"

Nodding to the Winchester, I replied, "That saddle gun does just as good a job. Better, sometimes."

FW Red opened his mouth to speak, hesitated, shrugged, and said, "All I can say is that you're one in a thousand out in this part of the country."

"Maybe so, but I wasn't born in the woods to be scared of an owl." I nodded to his cattle. "What about your stock?"

He glanced into the darkness south of us. "Only five or six head. If they're still there in the morning, I'll push them in."

"If they're not?"

His irrepressible grin broadened. "Then I'll ride in alone."

Neither of us slept much that night. Every sound jerked us from our soogans, whether it was the splashing of a fish, the passing of a deer, the rooting of an armadillo, or the rhythmic hooting of the barred owl. Most of the sounds I recognized, but there were some that kept me on the edge.

Over the years, I'd developed a knack for sleeping in the saddle, which never makes for a comfortable nap. That night, waiting for the Comanche was worse than any saddle nap I had ever taken.

Chapter Two

Next morning, upon FW Red's insistence, which I didn't fight any too hard, I rode out with him. I was running low on funds, and even if I couldn't get any pay, maybe I could find me a few days of found and keep. Besides, behind us, or maybe in front of us, were the Comanche.

FW Red was a talker. He never did run down. He started jabbering when we pulled out, and didn't stop until we came in sight of the Bar F. I wouldn't have been surprised if that old boy couldn't have argued a gopher out of its hole. At the same time, he kept his few head of stock moving and even picked up a few more before we reached the ranch.

"Not a bad-looking spread," I drawled, taking in the stone buildings and rugged corrals.

"Yep. The old man's name is Pete French," he

said as we reined up a half mile from the main
house and watched the beeves drift on in. "He came
here thirty or so years back—in the forties. Worked
his rear off, still does. Good man. Ornery as all get
out. Gripey and fussy, but one to ride the river
with." He hesitated, then looked around at me, his
eyes glittering with excitement. "I got me an idea.
Why don't you come to work for us? Pete can always use a good hand."

I shrugged, deciding not to mention that I had been
pondering that same notion. "Well, I don't know,
FW Red. I was planning on moving on to Uvalde."

"Ah, that can wait. Come on."

"Well, maybe. Let's see."

We rode on in.

The stock drifted into the grazing herd. Off to the
right was the Rio Frio. On either side spread luxuriant meadows of thick green grass almost belly-
high to my pony. FW Red was right; the old man
had built a fine spread.

As we drew closer, I spotted activity in one of
the several corrals. A handful of cowpokes was
clustered around the rails, watching a buster try to
tame a squealing stallion.

FW Red shouted, "That's O.C.! He's trying to
ride old Bill Quantrell. That horse is full of snake
poison."

Even from a distance, I could see the buster was
losing the battle. With each jump, more and more
daylight showed between the saddle and the cow-

poke's rear until finally, the cowpoke came down and the saddle wasn't there to catch him.

A round of catcalls and hoorahs greeted the disgusted cowboy who angrily slapped the dust from his chaps with his John B. "He got you that time, O.C."

A feminine voice called out, "Maybe you oughta hug his neck, O.C."

FW Red pointed to the young woman perched on the top rail, what they call the opera rail. She wore men's clothes. "That's the old man's youngest girl, Louisa. She's a keeper. Pure old tomboy, but she's a dandy. That youngster next to her is Little Pete, the old man's youngest."

The buster ignored her hoorah-ing. He just shook his head and climbed through the rails. "One of you jokers give him a try if you can do any better," he yelled back at his compadres as he stopped at the water bucket and filled a dipper with cold, sweet water.

A skinny jasper, not even as big around as one of the corral posts, shouted at a stocky cowpoke sitting on the opera rail on the other side of Miss Louisa, "Hey, Coco. Give old Bill Quantrell a try."

Coco shook his head, but the other wranglers egged him on. He threw up his hands in disgust. "All right, I do it. But, you boys, if this man-killer, he throw me off, you get me out. You hear?"

We reined up just outside the corral. I had a brief chance to study the black stallion. He was a big horse, sixteen, maybe even seventeen, hands with a blocky head and close-set eyes. I had the feeling that a devil's rage filled the animal. I had seen animals like him, killers. The unfortunate side of the story was they weren't born killers. Someone or something had made them that way through no fault of their own.

One cowpoke was holding the stallion's head and biting down on one of the ears as Coco swung into the saddle. In the next instant, a cloud of dust exploded. The cowpoke biting the ear came flying out one side, and Bill Quantrell came boiling out the other side for two or three lengths, then sunfished higher than I had ever seen a horse leap. He landed hard, then bucked high again, this time twisting his other side to the sun. He squealed and slammed into the ground, jarring the buster's teeth. One boot slipped out of a stirrup.

Instantly, the stallion went high again, showing his other side to the sun. He slammed to the ground. Daylight showed under Coco's seat as he lost his other stirrup. The stallion squealed. I could see the hate in his eyes. The hair on the back of my neck bristled.

In a flash, the stallion spun left, then right. He tossed another dazzling sunfish, slammed down hard, and spun, sending Coco tumbling to the ground.

That's when I grabbed my reata. FW Red frowned at me, but I paid him no attention.

The stunned cowboy lay motionless.

The enraged animal charged to the rails, spilling

the cowpokes from the opera rail. Then he spun, nostrils flared, his black mane flying, his teeth bared. Spying the cowpoke sprawled on the ground, he squealed, reared, and charged.

Cowboys shouted.

I whipped the reata over my head two times, then laid out a small loop that settled over Bill Quantrell's head fifteen feet before he reached the downed man.

Quickly, I dallied one end around the saddle horn and backed my horse Bill up. "Hold on, Boy," I muttered between gritted teeth. "This ain't going to be no church social."

The stallion hit the end of the rope and flipped upside down, almost jerking us off our feet. The stallion scrambled to his feet, but before he could gain any purchase, I backed up, dragging him to the rail and pinning him to it.

Then he started pulling.

I jerked the reins back, and Bill dropped his rear and stiffened his front feet, digging into the hardpan. He grunted and jerked back on the rope, which stretched so tight it vibrated. Bill pulled the black back against the rails.

Two cowhands jumped in the corral and hauled the stunned buster out the gate while a third grabbed the stallion's hackamore. Between the cowpoke and Bill, we held the stallion. As soon as Coco was safely from the corral, I loosened the rope and the one called O.C. slipped the loop off the stallion's neck.

An old man strode toward me, shaking his head. "Mighty fine piece of roping, Mister. Much obliged. You saved Coco's hide. Names's Pete French. This here is my spread."

Rolling up the reata, I nodded. "Mine's Lew Hobbs. Glad to be of help, Mister French."

"Pete," he replied. He was a short, square man who appeared to have been heavily muscled in his youth, but now as the tooth grew longer, fat had come to replace the muscle. His blue eyes twinkled in appreciation. "Yes, Sir. Why you must've snaked that loop out there thirty-forty feet. Don't see much of that no more."

Behind him, a taller hombre with a lantern jaw and cold eyes curled his lips but remained silent.

Pete continued, "Climb down off that Cayuse and be welcome to supper."

I didn't need to be asked twice. I tied my lasso to the saddle and swung down.

The old man offered me his hand. I introduced myself.

"And this here is Bart Runnels, my range boss," he said, hooking a thumb over his shoulder at the lantern-jawed jasper.

"Howdy." I nodded to the surly man.

Runnels gave me a brief, almost imperceptible nod, his eyes taking in the fact I wore no sidearm. Then he spoke to the old man. "I told you about that man-killer, Pete. I say we get rid of him before he kills somebody." He gestured to a cowpoke no bigger around than a fencepost hobbling toward the barn. "Needle is still limping from that killer slamming him into the rails yesterday, and we're lucky Coco didn't get hisself stomped to a grease spot. We get all our busters hurt, you ain't going to be able to fill your contract with the Army."

I looked at the stallion. O.C. still held the hackamore. The stallion stood just beyond the rails staring at us, eyes wide, ears laid back. *Yep,* I told myself. *That one is mean.*

French shook his head. "I don't know, Runnels. There's sure devil enough in that animal, but I never cottoned to killing animals."

Runnels snorted.

The old man looked up at me. "You done any busting?"

I shrugged. "Some."

He glanced at the coiled rope dangling from my saddle and studied me a moment as if he was trying to make up his mind about me. "What do you reckon? The stallion worth keeping?"

For several moments, I considered the animal. He appeared to possess just about every physical attribute a jasper could want in a horse. The only problem was temperament, and unfortunately that counted for about seventy-five percent of a animal's worth. "Hard to say. He's a tough ride, a real booger."

Runnels glared at me. "You think you could ride that jughead?" The tone in his voice and the look in his eyes dared me to try.

Sensing his animosity, I shook my head slowly, still studying the black. "Like I said, he's a real booger."

Runnels grinned. "I didn't think so." He called out, "O.C. Take the saddle off that hammerhead and tie him to the rail. I'll get my Winchester."

I always figured what I said next was because I had taken an instant dislike to Bart Runnels. My words stopped him in his tracks. "But yes, I can ride him." FW Red looked around at me in surprise. I grinned and winked at him.

Pete French stepped forward. "Ain't no need for that, Hobbs. That critter is a bad one. Runnels is right in all likelihood. Best we get rid of him."

With a nod of appreciation to the old man for his concern, I pulled my gloves from my hip pocket and tugged them on. "Give me a hand, boys," I said, climbing up the rails.

FW Red crawled through the rails and took the hackamore from O.C. Moving slowly, I climbed down and eased toward the nervous horse. "Give me the rope and hold tight to the bosal while I climb aboard."

The stallion tried to look back at me with those rolling eyes, but FW Red held his head tight. I took the rope in my right hand and grabbed an ear with my left to distract him while I swung into the saddle.

I hit the saddle and the black busted loose, sending FW Red scrambling for the rails. Squealing, the enraged stallion spun left, then right. I hung tight, the muscles in my arm strumming like steel bands to keep the rope taut.

Ears back, he reared high, then dropped, kicking his hind feet high into the air, trying to throw me over his head. I fought for balance, shifting my shoulders backward. When his back feet hit the ground, I jerked forward, an instant before he sprinted ten yards, hoping to roll me off his back. Bellowing, he went into the sunfishing leaps I had seen earlier, the ones that had popped the other busters from the saddle.

He sunfished to the right, throwing his left side toward the sun. "Okay, fella," I muttered. "Give me your twist." And he did, to the right, then a sunfish to the left followed by his trademark twist.

That was the move that had broken Coco and O.C. loose, but I had managed to keep my legs tight about his belly, my rear plastered to the saddle. My head popped and jerked as his sharp, abrupt moves snapped me forward and back. My John B. flew off my head, and the wind whipped my hair.

Squealing in anger and frustration at the clinging tick on his back, the stallion shot high into the air and came down on all four feet, crushing me into the saddle. Then he went into a frenzy of jumps, coming down harder after each one than the one before.

From somewhere distant I heard shouts and cheers, but they were almost smothered by the pounding in my ears, water sloshing in the stallion's belly, and his expulsion of wind with each jump.

I lost count of the number of times we circled the corral, his jumps slowing with each circuit. Finally, he stopped and stood motionless, his head drooping, his sleek black body covered with foamy white lather.

I remained in the saddle, leaning forward and rubbing his neck. "Easy, Boy. You done good. Just take it easy. Things get better now."

Slowly, deliberately, I swung one leg over the saddle, and for several seconds I remained standing in the single stirrup before settling myself back in the saddle. I repeated the little exercise two or three times before lowering myself to the ground.

I glanced across the corral at Pete French. "This here pony is too good to shoot." I glanced at Runnels. "He just needs more work." I handed the rope to O.C. "Walk him around to cool off. Keep him off water until he is."

Pete French met me outside the corral. With a broad grin, he shook his head. "You okay, Boy?"

Rolling my shoulders, I replied, "Reckon I might have a few bolts and screws jarred loose, but for the most, I'm in one piece."

The old man's grin grew wider. "Well, Son, it appears you can ride as well as you can rope. You looking for a job?"

I took my hat from FW Red and dusted it off against my leg. "What about the black?"

He arched an eyebrow. "You stay and work with him?"

With a grin, I replied, "That being the case, I don't reckon I would turn a job down, Mister French."

He grabbed my hand and shook it hard. "Twenty dollars a month and keep. And you'll earn ever penny of it."

Several other cowpokes had gathered round, congratulating me on the ride. A youngster around twelve or so pushed through the crowd. He looked up at me with a big grin on his freckled face. "That was the best doggone riding I ever saw, Mister."

"Why thank you, Son. What's your name?"

"I'm Little Pete, and I sure would like for you to teach me to ride like that."

The cowpokes around us laughed. One patted Little Pete on the shoulder. "You got to grow some more, Sprout," he said, teasing the boy good-naturedly.

Keeping his eyes on me, Little Pete shrugged the hand off. "Will you, Mister Hobbs? Will you? Huh?"

I grinned at him and nodded. "You need a few more inches and pounds, Little Pete. Then we'll see." I glanced beyond the cluster and saw Runnels and three other cowpokes glaring at me. They looked away when our eyes met. I had a feeling I'd made some enemies.

Chapter Three

That evening in the chuck house, we plopped down at a table laden with platters of fried steaks, heaping bowls of succotash, steaming red-eye gravy, and hot sourdough biscuits fresh from the spider.

FW Red motioned me to sit by him. It was only after we had all bellied up to the table that I noticed Runnels and his three compadres—Joe Carson, Ike Bailey, and Frank Barton—had taken seats at the far end of the table. I paid them little attention, but I couldn't help noticing throughout the meal that the little group spoke only to each other in whispers.

Now I might not be too bright, but at least I know enough not to spit upwind, so it wasn't hard for me to figure out that there were two factions among the ranch hands.

Clearing his throat, Needle spoke up. "That was some fancy riding, Hobbs. Whereabouts you from?"

I paused before taking a bite of steak smothered with gravy. "All over," I replied, deliberately avoiding his question.

Needle grimaced. "Didn't intend to pry."

Around a mouthful of grub, FW Red said, "How'd you manage to stay on that outlaw? Nobody else has been able to do it."

I glanced at Runnels, who was paying me no attention in a mighty deliberate sort of way. "Lucky, I reckon." I sipped my coffee. "Has the black been around here long?"

"Too long," Runnels growled. "That jarhead is mean clean through."

Coco spoke up. "Me, I think we get him two, maybe three weeks with that last herd we bring in from the Nueces." He shook his bald head emphatically. "There be nice herds of mustangs around the Nueces."

I simply nodded, not wanting to say too much, for it was obvious Runnels had no use at all for the black, nor for me.

Runnels continued, "You didn't do the old man no favors when you rode that horse, Cowboy. He's a killer, and the thing you do with killers is shoot them before them stomp a buster to pieces." He glared at me, his cold eyes daring me to disagree.

With what I hoped was a disarming grin, I

shrugged. "Either kill them or turn them loose to maintain the quality of the wild mustangs."

Frank Barton looked at me from under his bushy eyebrows and snorted. "I wouldn't give that man-killer the satisfaction of turning him loose."

"Your choice," I replied around a mouthful of grub.

"You're right there," growled Joe Carson, shoving his Montana-crowned hat to the back of his head. The third hombre, Ike Bailey, stared at me with cold eyes.

Needle nodded in the direction of my waist. "I notice you don't carry a sidearm. Sometimes they come in mighty useful out here."

If I'd been asked the question once, I'd been asked it a hundred times. "I have my saddle gun. It does me just fine." I didn't tell them that I knew from experience if you wore a sidearm, you were more likely to use it. Instead, I added, "Besides, sometimes it helps you stay out of trouble."

Runnels snorted. Carson leaned forward. With a sneer on his lips, he said, "Some people might think a jasper not wearing one was scared."

The tension at the table became palpable. I grinned easily. "Reckon so, Carson, but that could be a big mistake on their part."

His eyes narrowed. "You saying—"

I don't know where the conversation might have gone from there, but Little Pete came bursting through the door, gasping for breath after all his running, his eyes filled with excitement. "Pa wants to see you up at the house, Mister Hobbs."

Frowning, I glanced at the other cowpokes. As one, they all fit a crooked smirk on their faces. Puzzled by the unexpected request and my bunkmates' odd behavior, I looked around at Little Pete. "Now?"

He nodded. "Yes, Sir. If you don't mind."

I glanced at Runnels and his three compadres. If looks could have killed, I'd of been dead more times than a cat. "I don't mind," I replied, downing the rest of my coffee.

FW Red snickered. I frowned at him. "Something wrong?"

O.C. and Coco grinned. "You'll see," O.C. answered.

"Naw, nothing ain't wrong," Needle chimed in. "Go on. You'll see."

To my surprise, Mister French led me into the parlor and introduced me to his wife, Marlene. "I told Mrs. French about you, Hobbs, and she wanted to meet you."

Holding my hat in front of me with both hands, I nodded awkwardly, wondering just why in the blazes a lady like her would want to meet a threadbare drifter like me. "Ma'am."

She offered me her hand. "Very pleased to meet you, Mister Hobbs." She nodded to a steaming pot on the table in front of the couch. "Would you care for some coffee?"

I glanced at the old man. He nodded for me to accept her offer, and that's when I noticed a strange gleam in his eyes as well as a tiny grin on his face. "Why, yes, Ma'am. I'd be pleased."

She nodded to a chair. "Please have a seat," she said as she poured the coffee and handed me my cup, one of those dainty little china cups that felt like a thimble in my gnarled hand. After filling her own cup, she gingerly sat on the couch across the table from me. She looked me up and down. "My husband tells me you seem to have a way with horses."

Self-conscious of my frayed duds, I tried to draw my dusty boots back under me as I nodded and sipped my coffee. "Yes, Ma'am." All the while I was wondering where this was leading.

"You from Texas, Mister Hobbs?"

"Yes, Ma'am."

"What brings you down here?"

If a man had come out and asked me that question, I'd of told him it was none of his business, but a woman is different, so I made up a little story I thought would rest easy on a woman's delicate ears. And she seemed satisfied. She asked a heap more questions and I just kept answering them, though at times I did glance at Mister French who was leaning against the wall behind his wife, nodding to me.

Finally she must have grown tired of asking questions, for then she started telling me about her family and got around to their children—Alicia, Louisa, and Little Pete.

"Since you're going to be working for us, I thought you might like to meet the children. Little Pete you've already met." She turned her head toward an open door. "Girls, come in here, please." She turned back to me, and with a matronly smile on her round cheeks, said, "This is Alicia—she's the oldest—and Louisa."

I almost dropped my cup of coffee when the two young ladies walked in, both dressed in fetching calico dresses. "Girls, I want you to meet Mister Hobbs, our newest employee."

Employee? That was the first time I'd heard a cowpuncher called an employee.

Cup and saucer in hand, I jumped to my feet and nodded awkwardly to the young women. The older one was right pretty, and trim the way a lady needed to be trim. She was the kind cowpokes only dream about. I had to swallow the dry lump in my throat. "Ladies." I remained motionless, having absolutely no idea what I should do next. I glanced uncomfortably at the beckoning doorway.

The younger one, Miss Louisa, as the busters called her, stepped forward with a bright smile on her face and stuck out her hand. "Very pleased to meet you, Mister Hobbs. I saw you ride the black this afternoon. That was some of the best blasted ridin'—"

"Louisa!" her mother snapped. "Watch your language. We don't want Mister Hobbs to think we're not proper folk."

Miss Louisa rolled her eyes. "Oh, Mama! Well,

I still think that was the best ride I've ever seen, Mister Hobbs."

I shifted the saucer and cup to my left hand, took her hand, and nodded, feeling my ears burn and the blush come to my cheeks. "Thank you, Ma'am." I glanced at her sister, hoping she was going to say something.

She did, but not what I expected. She lifted a disapproving eyebrow at her sister. "You're such a child, Louisa." Then she gave me a faint smile. "Very pleased to meet you, Mister Hobbs."

"Thank you. Me too. I mean, meeting you," I added awkwardly.

For a few moments we stood, staring at each other. I shifted around on my feet, growing more and more nervous. I suppose Mrs. French saw she had a Mexican standoff, so she promptly rose and said, "That's enough, Girls. It's getting late. Say your prayers. Pa and I will see Mister Hobbs out."

With Bull Durham cigarettes dangling from their lips, the boys were squatting on the ground with their backs against the bunkhouse when I got back. The grins that were plastered to their faces when I left were even wider now.

"Well," FW Red called out. "How'd it go?"

The others tried to suppress their laughter.

With a helpless shrug, I replied, "How'd it go about what? I'm not any too sure just why Mister French invited me up there. His wife did all the talking."

Their laughter erupted. "And you got to meet the daughters, huh?" Needle asked.

Suddenly I had an inkling of the purpose of the visit, but I shoved it aside as crazier than a loco bedbug. "Yep, but I don't know why."

Coco shook his head. "My friend, you don't know women."

I had to admit I didn't. "So?"

"So," O.C. replied. "Mrs. French was sizing you up as a husband for one of her girls."

All I could do was stare down at their grinning faces.

Needle explained, "Almost every cowpoke passing by gets invited in for coffee. She's deathly afraid the girls will end up spinsters, so she's trying to hitch them up with a spry young stallion," he added, a lecherous grin on his face.

I shook my head. "That's bull. Nobody in her right mind would hitch up fine young ladies like those two with a beaten-down drifter like me with no future, and no promises for no future." But to be honest, the idea, as outrageous as it might seem, lodged itself in my head. Maybe it could work.

O.C. started another cigarette. "No? Well, Sunday will tell."

"What are you talking about?"

Needle spoke up. "If they invite you to Sunday dinner, then that means you made a good impression."

I looked at FW Red. He nodded and tossed me

his bag of Bull Durham. "That's right. Sunday you'll know where you stand. Here. Have a smoke."

They kidded me a few more minutes.

While I would never had admitted it to those fellers, I was kind of flattered that Mrs. French would even consider an ugly jasper like me a proper man for one of the girls. And if I had a choice, the older one, Alicia, would be it. Despite myself, I sure was looking forward to Sunday.

We smoked in silence, each with his own thoughts. FW Red glanced at the starry sky and remarked, "Getting chilly."

Needle grunted. "Always does."

I cleared my throat. "FW Red. That's an unusual handle. How'd you come by it?"

O.C. chuckled. "Go ahead and tell him, FW Red."

Coco joined in the laughter.

"You boys hush up," FW Red shot back.

"Go ahead. You tell him or we will," O.C. threatened.

With feigned resignation, FW Red shook his head and muttered, "I reckon if I don't, you old boys will just keep hounding me." He sighed deeply and began, "Well, I used to go by just Red, but once, me and some old boys was up in Fort Worth. And, ah, we was having us a good old time, visiting all the bars and making pests of ourselves at some of the escort establishments, if you know what I mean. Well, Sir, I spotted this lady of the evening in a fine dress on the sidewalk all by herself, standing just outside a saloon, and since the streets were full of soiled doves, I took her for one." He hesitated.

"Go on," said Coco. "Here's where it gets good, Hobbs."

Having second thoughts, FW Red shook his head, then decided to continue. "Ah, what the Sam Hill. Anyway, I swooped down on her, grabbed her about her tiny waist, and planted a big kiss on those cherry-red lips. Next thing I knew, I was lying in the middle of the street with the sheriff standing over me wanting to know just what in the blazes I was doing taking advantage of his baby daughter."

Coco, O.C., and Needles broke into braying laughter. "Go ahead." O.C. laughed. "Tell him what happened next."

Before FW Red could utter a syllable, Needles chimed in, "Sheriff made him strip off his pants and ride out of town in his longjohns. That's where he got his handle, Fort Worth Red."

The three cowpokes rolled over on their sides from laughter while FW Red just shook his head and reached for the bag of Bull Durham.

The whinny of a horse caught my attention. I looked around at the dark shadow of the barn in time to see a single rider head out toward the river.

Neither FW Red nor the three cowpokes still rolling on the ground paid the rider any attention. While I figured it was a right curious happening, no one else seemed concerned. I just shrugged and rolled another cigarette.

Chapter Four

Next morning, Runnels sent Needle and me south to check on the stock between the ranch and the line camp where we would spend the night. Some cows were still dropping little ones, and French wanted a rough count of both cows and wild horses. Although he was pushing a herd to the army within a few days, he had another shipment of horses scheduled for next month, and he wanted to make certain they were available. FW Red and O.C. rode north on the same task.

As we ambled out of the ranch yard, Needle drawled, "Ain't often I been down this way. Usually, I go back north. We'll have to keep our eyes peeled. I don't know all the hiding spots down this way like I do back north."

I frowned at him. "What do you mean?"

He glanced around. When he spotted the confused frown on my face, he chuckled. "Nothing. Just jawing. We usually work the same pastures and canyons. That way, we find all the hiding spots where we might overlook some stock."

I nodded. That made sense.

Overhead, distant specks glided through the brittle blue sky. The perfume of wild honeysuckle lay on the still air like a feather quilt, and the bright green grass of the meadows contrasted with the chalky white bluffs of the canyon. It was the kind of day made for a cowboy on his horse—open spaces and nothing to stop an hombre from riding beyond whichever horizon he chose.

Needle kept up a running chatter about the ranch and the stock. "Yes, Sir. The old man probably runs a couple thousand head through here. We done already sold a few hundred to trail herds heading up the old Shawnee Trail to the Chisholm."

Out of habit, I kept my eyes moving, searching the strange but beautiful country around me. "Runnels talked about a herd of horses for the Army. Does Mister French sell the remounts on a regular basis?"

Needle shrugged. "I don't know about regular, but every time we bust thirty or forty head, we run them up to Camp Verde."

"Runnels been range boss long?"

A crooked grin curled Needle's lips. "Longer than I like to think about."

Keeping my eyes quartering the country around us, I asked, "What's going on at the ranch?"

From the corner of my eye, I saw the lanky cowpoke glance around at me. He hesitated. "What do you mean?"

I shrugged. "Like at supper last night. Runnels and those three sat all by their lonesome, just like the rest of us had just come in from the hog pen."

He snorted. "Runnels hired them three. They all hang together closer than a dozen cowpokes in one bunk. I don't know if Runnels knew them from the old days or what, but they don't talk to the rest of us much. Right from the beginning, they left us alone." He wrinkled his long face into a frown. "Which is okay with me."

Where the canyon narrowed and the river grew swifter, we paused to let our ponies drink. We climbed down and sipped the icy water. Needle dragged the back of his hand across his lips. "No finer sweet water anywhere else." He grinned.

I agreed. Sweet and cold. I removed my hat and splashed icy water in my face and ran my fingers through my short-cropped hair. For the first time since I had left Madison in East Texas, I felt comfortable, like I was at home. I leaned forward for another drink.

That's when the slugs slammed into the rocky shoreline, one less than a foot from my head.

Needle shouted. I jumped to my feet and, as the next shot echoed across the canyon, swung into the saddle even as Bill was breaking for the shelter of the oak and pecan. Leaning low over my pony's neck, I kept my eyes forward as I snaked the Winchester from the boot.

I heard the boom of a rifle followed by the splat of a slug smashing into the rocky ground.

We hit the tree line and I leaped from the saddle, landing behind a thick oak. Needle crouched behind a nearby pecan. He shouted, "Where in the Sam Hill did that come from?"

Jamming the butt of the Winchester into my shoulder, I nodded to the rim of the canyon beyond the river. "Up yonder."

Puffs of smoke appeared on the rim. Whoever up there was using older rifles, black powder rifles. The telltale smoke was a dead giveaway for a shooter's location, the main reason I had dumped my black powder guns and bought me one of those Yellowboy Henrys just after they came out back in '61, and later a Winchester in '66.

"You see 'em? You see 'em?" Needle shouted, panic and fear in his voice.

"I told you. Up on the rim." I found a puff of smoke, settled the front sights of the Winchester on it, and waited. Memories of the war came flooding back. How many times had I been in a spot just like this? I shook my head, clearing it of distracting thoughts, and focused on the present. I tightened the pressure on the trigger and waited. Moments later there came another puff, and I instantly squeezed off a shot.

Seconds later, a distant cry echoed across the canyon and a dark figure tumbled head over heels to the rocky ground below.

Immediately, I shifted the muzzle toward the second shooter and squeezed off a shot. I muttered a curse even as the Winchester fired. Too much to the left.

Moments later, a figure jumped to his feet, but before I could get off another shot, he disappeared.

Needle stared at me in disbelief. "How in the blazes did you do that? I ain't never seen shooting like that."

I slid fresh cartridges in the magazine. "Not all that good. I missed the second one."

He gave a short laugh. "I ain't talking about the second. It was the first."

"Luck," I said, swinging into the saddle with my Winchester in hand and dismissing the conversation. "Now, let's ride over there and see who our friend is."

He was pure Comanche—glistening black hair, broad cheekbones, skin bronzed by the sun. I couldn't help feeling a tinge of sorrow when I looked down on the lean, muscular body of a man who should have lived and enjoyed life for years longer. I could never understand what it was in a man that made him kill and ravage. I knew it was inherent in the Comanche culture, but I could never fathom such beliefs and traditions.

Needle rolled the Comanche's head to one side with the toe of his boot and shook his head. "The bottom of the throat. Busted his spine." He kicked the dead Indian. "Serves him right." He drew back his foot to kick the limp body again.

"No," I said, softly but with steel. "I ain't explaining nothing, but we're burying him."

Needle looked at me as if I were loco. "Burying? An Injun?"

I fixed my eyes on his. "If someone kills you, do you want to lie out there and have wolves and coyotes tear you up?"

He paused, staring down at his feet. "Makes no difference. You're dead, you're dead."

I climbed down and slid my Winchester back in the boot. "Well, maybe makes no difference to you, but it does to me. I'll bury him."

He glanced around, sudden alarm in his eyes. "What about the others?"

"Gone. Weren't many. Maybe only the two."

The lanky cowpoke nodded. He stepped aside as I straightened the body and stacked stones over him. After a few minutes, he joined in. I said nothing, just kept working.

Within ten minutes, the body was covered. I stepped back and surveyed our work. "Well," I drawled. "We did the best we could."

Needle looked at me, a curious expression on his

face. "You really believe them Comanches would do the same thing for you?"

I shrugged and swung back into the saddle. "Probably not. That's the difference between them and civilized folk."

For a moment, the lanky cowpoke studied on my answer. "I ain't never thought about it like that." He paused, his forehead wrinkled in concentration. "I reckon you could be right."

By the end of the day, we had tallied over nine hundred head of fat cows and sassy calves, as well as thirty or forty frisky mustangs that bolted back up the canyons and up onto the rims when they spotted us.

We rode up on one of the rims after them just to see where they were headed. I reined up on the rim and peered out over the lush canyons and valleys of the Frio. It was a mighty pretty scene: luxuriant valleys nestled below in the canyons, hundreds of acres of thick grass nourished by the supply of sweet water from the Frio. I supposed the Garden of Eden might have looked like that.

We spent the night at the line shack, a small but well-built rock cabin. Over a supper of fish caught fresh from the Frio, I learned the origin of Needle's nickname.

"Well," he drawled. "I was always skinny. One day, my old man looked at me and said, 'You know, Boy. You're so skinny that if you closed one eye, you'd look like a needle,' and I been stuck with it every since."

I laughed. "Stand up and close one eye," I said. "Let me see for myself."

Next morning we crossed the river and headed back, taking our time. Needle reined up and climbed off his pony. "I think he's picked up a rock," he said, lifting his horse's front left foot up between his knees. With his pocketknife, he popped the stone from under the shoe and studied the animal's foot.

"Bad?"

He gave his head a sharp nod. "Bruised. Looks bad." He muttered a curse. "And just when we were going up on the rim."

"The rim?"

"Yep." He pointed up the canyon. "As I recollect, ahead is a trail that stock sometimes wanders up to the rim. We usually find a few head up there and drive 'em back down, but I don't cotton none to making this animal climb up that rocky trail."

"I'll go," I replied. "Stay here and give your pony a rest. If I find any Bar F stock up there, I'll drive them down."

Needle ground-reined his horse and reached for his bag of Bull Durham. "You ain't getting no argument from me."

The trail was wide enough for three or four riders side-by-side. Fresh cow patties among the dry ones were mute evidence that the trail was heavily used.

Once on the rim, I spotted a few head grazing some distance away on the side of a rolling hill. Bill had always had a knack chasing down cows, so within minutes, we had five or six heading down the trail. Once I felt they would keep going, I turned back to search for more.

Below in the canyon and valleys, the vegetation was lush and thick, but on the rim, it was stunted and twisted. Cedar and scrubby mesquite grew thick on the rolling hills beyond the rim. I reined up on the crest of a hill and scanned the country to the west.

Far to the south, three muffled gunshots drifted across the rolling hills. Instantly alert, I peered toward the sound, but saw nothing. After several minutes, I turned back to rounding up stray cows.

I spotted some grazing to the west, which I quickly rounded up and headed back. For another hour I roamed the rim, working farther and farther south, sending at least forty or fifty head back down.

"Pull up, Bill," I muttered, tugging gently on the reins and squinting once again in the direction of the gunshots. "Let's take another look."

As far as I could see, not a living creature stirred except a single redtail hawk gliding on the rising heat and a few vultures circling ominously to the south. Just as I started to rein around, I spotted a lone figure top out on a hill some half-mile distant, coming from the general direction of the earlier gunfire.

Instinctively, I backed Bill down the hill far enough so I could peer over the crest. The rider continued in my direction. Unless he changed his course, he would pass a hundred yards or so west of me.

As the rider grew closer, I recognized the Montana crown. "Carson," I muttered to myself, remembering the single cowpoke who had ridden out from the ranch two nights earlier.

At the time I'd paid no attention, but now that I put my mind to it, I couldn't recollect seeing the surly cowboy the morning after, the morning Needle and me rode out. I glanced north in the direction of the ranch. And best I could figure, he would have been hard-pressed to ride out this morning, get this far, and then turn back.

Carson drew closer. I eased Bill to the side, keeping the hill between us. I glanced over my shoulder at the vultures. I was as curious as a pup with his first porcupine.

After Carson had passed, I headed south, directly for the vultures. I stayed in the valleys between the hills, not wanting to top out against the skyline.

An hour later, I rode around the base of a hill and jerked my pony to a halt. The beating of great wings broke the silence of the hot afternoon. A dozen vultures lumbered into the sky, leaving the remains of a cowpoke and his horse.

The dun horse had been shot in the head. I

couldn't tell about the cowpoke for the vultures had done a pretty fair job on him.

I knelt and gingerly searched his pockets for some indication who the poor jasper might be, but his pockets had been picked cleaner than a new mirror, and his holster was empty. I glanced around, and a shiny reflection behind a new cedar caught my attention.

It was a Colt handgun. I picked it up and read the initials on the butt, J.B.A.

For several moments, I pondered my next move. Behind me, Bill whinnied. "What is it, Boy?" I laid my hand on the reins. His attention seemed to focus on the southwest. Was someone else headed this way?

I couldn't take the chance. "Sorry, Cowboy," I said as I shoved the six-gun in my saddlebag and climbed onto the saddle. "I'll come back later and bury you."

On the ride back to Needle, I turned the events of the last hour or so over in my mind. Carson had ridden out two nights earlier. Now I had seen him coming from the direction in which I found a dead man and his horse.

Was Carson part of it? Why was he out here? Where had he been for the last two days?

I paused at the top of the rim and looked in the direction of the ranch. Ever since the boys had told me about a possible invitation to Sunday dinner from the Frenches, the possibility had been in the back of my mind. I even let myself imagine what it would be like on the ranch with a fine woman like Miss Alicia.

As I headed down the trail, reality snapped me back to the present. "Don't kid yourself, Hobbs. She's too good for you," I warned myself. Still, dreams don't go away just because you tell them to.

Chapter Five

Joe Carson was squatting in the shade of a pecan tree with Needle when I rode up. I nodded, noting the Yellowboy Henry booted under his stirrup flap. "Howdy."

He glanced at the rim. "I just come down from up there. How come I didn't see you?"

I said nothing about the three gunshots. "Reckon because I didn't see you. I'd been looking for cattle back to the northwest," I added. "What are you doing out here? Runnels send you to check on us?" I grinned.

A frown twisted the edges of his lips down. "Just checking on things. That's all." He rose and swung into the saddle. "See you boys back at the ranch."

We watched Carson disappear among the oak and pecan. Needle shook his head. "That old boy was mighty curious about where you were and what you was doing. Yes, Siree. Wanting to know where you was, what you was doing, how long you'd been gone—all kinds of questions."

I thought about the dead man, and the hogleg with the initials, J.B.A. I glanced at Needle, then decided to bounce my questions off FW Red.

When we reached the ranch that evening, we reported to Runnels. The way he stared at me while Needle told him the condition and number of stock we had seen, I could tell he was wondering if I was doing anything else up on the rim besides popping beeves out of the cedar.

We locked eyes. I knew when he narrowed his that he realized I knew more than I let on.

"So you didn't see no Injuns or anything up there, huh?" His voice was a growl.

"Nope. Not a sight of one. Why, I didn't even see Carson who said he was up there, but then, I was way north." Another lie.

After supper, I ambled out to the corral where the black was kept. When he spotted me, his ears perked forward, then lay back. Teeth bared, he charged the rails, cutting sharply at the last second and racing around the perimeter of the corral, lowering his head and lashing out with his hind feet.

The moon was full, lighting the corrals and barns like the sun. I rolled a cigarette and watched the black's antics in amusement. Just before I touched a match to the cigarette, the smell of fresh soap drifted past me. I glanced around to see Miss Louisa and Little Pete approaching.

Having shed her pants for a dress, Miss Louisa smiled brightly and nodded to the black. "He doesn't like you, Mister Hobbs."

"Call me Lew." I cupped the match to the end of the cigarette. "No, I reckon he doesn't. It's hard to like someone who bests you. But he'll get better. With enough work, he should make your pa a fine cowpony."

Little Pete bubbled, "When are you going to teach me to ride like you, Mist—I mean, Lew? Huh?"

I glanced down at his animated face. "Maybe come Sunday, we can talk about it some more. I studied his thin frame. "If your pa doesn't mind, maybe we can put you on a calf or two."

He clapped his hands. "Whoopee!"

Miss Louisa shook her head, her short brown hair bobbing from side to side. "You'll break your neck, Peter John," she said in stern voice.

"Oh, you don't know nothing, Sis."

"Peter John!"

"Well, you don't."

Not wanting to be the trigger for a family war, I changed the subject. "Your pa has built himself a right fine ranch here."

Before Miss Louisa could reply, Little Pete spoke

up. "I'll be running it one day. When I do, I'll fire Runnels and make you range boss, Lew. I don't like him."

"Hush that kind of talk, Pete," Miss Louisa barked. "Pa'll tan your hide."

He stuck out his jaw. "It's the truth."

I remembered that morning, Carson coming from the direction of the dead jasper. I remembered the gunshots. Innocently, I said, "Runnels seems like a fair man to me. He must be pretty good at his job for your pa to keep him on."

Chastised by my remark, Little Pete clamped his mouth shut. Miss Louisa nodded. "He's been with Pa three years now. Pa needed him because of the horse-stealing."

"Horse-stealing?"

"Cows too," Little Pete volunteered.

Miss Louisa explained, "It was about three years ago. Our range boss, Jim Winters, was bushwhacked and a herd of horses was stolen. Pa hired Runnels. He didn't stop all the Comanche raids, but most of them."

"Comanche, huh?"

"Yeah," Little Pete replied. "When I grow up, I'm going to hunt every last Comanche down and make him a good Indian."

"Don't talk like that, Peter John. It isn't Christian."

I took a drag on my cigarette and blew a stream

of smoke into the air. "You say your pa is still losing stock?"

"Yes. But not like he did before Runnels took over as the range boss."

Before I could ask any further questions, a feminine voice carried through the night from the main house, "Louisa, Peter John. Time to come in."

Later in the bunkhouse, I told FW Red about the dead man.

He frowned at the six-gun. "J.B.A.?" He shook his head. "I don't know of anyone around here with those initials. 'Course, it might be someone over to Uvalde. What are you going to do with it?"

I shrugged and wrapped a neckerchief around the six-gun and slipped it back in my saddlebags. "Hold on to it until I can find someone who knows what the initials stand for, I reckon." Clearing my throat, I glanced over my shoulder at the other cowpokes. Some were playing poker. Others had already turned in for the night. "I hear there used to be a heap of rustling around here. Comanches?"

FW Red ran his fingers through his curly hair and shook his head in frustration. "They've been a plague, sure enough."

"Still going on?"

"Sometimes. Not nearly as much before Runnels and his boys got here." He glanced in Runnels's direction. "I don't like the man, but he's done a good job. And I reckon that's all that counts. The bottom line."

I agreed.

Next morning, we started busting horses for the next shipment to the army. Three corrals were in use. Runnels's boys worked one and FW Red and Coco the second, leaving me and Needle at the third.

The ponies were kept in a fourth corral, the trap corral. The fifth was empty, waiting for those we busted.

The Army paid thirty-five dollars for a broke re-mount, so we made sure we gave them their money's worth, which meant that after we green-broke the broomtails, we brought them back for two or three more rides. By then, most were gentled enough so that even the soldier boys could stay in the saddle. Occasionally, we'd run across a gut-twister that took an extra couple rides.

Even though we took turns busting, by the end of the day our insides felt like we'd taken them out and tossed them back in. We were so tired that we weren't even hungry, but we shoveled beans and bacon down our gullets and then gratefully fell into our bunks. The only thing that could have rolled us out of our soogans was a stampede.

The next day was a repeat of the first.

From six A.M. to noon, Needle and me took the kinks out of six broncos, and then took a much-needed break for dinner. After washing the dust off, I detoured by the bunkhouse for another bag of cigarette makings. I bent over for my saddlebags and froze. I glanced around the empty bunkhouse, then back at the leather bags. They had been moved. But was it deliberate, or simply the result of some cowpoke's big foot? At that moment, FW Red poked his head in the doorway. "Let's go, Hobbs. Those buzzards will gobble everything up if you don't hurry."

I unbuckled the bags, retrieved my Bull Durham, saw the hogleg, then shrugged. I chided myself for letting my imagination run away with me. When I reached the doorway, I jerked to a halt. The six-gun. I had wrapped it in a neckerchief when I put it away the night before. The neckerchief had been removed.

Glancing at the cowpokes piling into the rock building, I wondered if anyone was watching from inside. Without looking over my shoulder, I headed across the hardpan to the chuck house.

My mind wasn't on my job that afternoon. As a result, I lost my saddle a few times, much to Needle's glee. I had worked with a heap of cowpokes over the last few years, and the majority respected a man's bunk as one piece of earth not to be violated by others. It was one of many unwritten rules cowboys followed.

Yet someone had prowled through my plunder.

Mid-afternoon, I laid a neat loop over the head

of a high-kicking chestnut gelding. The rope snapped.

I headed for the tack room in the back of the barn for another, grousing and complaining under my breath. I didn't like new ropes. Too stiff. Maybe I could stumble across some that were already broken in.

While rummaging through the half-darkened room, I heard voices in the barn. I was reaching for a rope when I heard my name mentioned. Curious, I peered through a the small crack in the wall and spotted Runnels talking to Barton.

"I don't know who that Hobbs hombre is, but the .44 with the ranger's initials means he found the body." He cursed. "I told Carson to bury him. That dumb—"

Barton broke in. "He said he saw a rider coming. It might have been Hobbs."

Runnels shook his head. Even in the shadows of the barn, the malevolent grimace on his face was clearly obvious. "Makes no difference. I'm going to run Hobbs off. You just keep an eye on him this afternoon. Make sure he stays away from the bunk-house, you hear?" He jabbed Barton in the chest with his finger.

"Yeah, I hear," the cowpoke replied, rubbing his chest.

After they left, I grabbed a rope and went out a side door.

Runnels was up to something no good.

"About time you got back," Needle said. "I figured you was taking a nap or something."

I shook my head and played out my rope. "A nap
would be right good, but we got work to do." I laid
the loop over the chestnut's head and pulled him in.

An hour later while I was earing a frightened
pinto so Needle could swing into the saddle, I
caught a glimpse of Runnels entering the bunkhouse. Moments later, he came out and casually
sauntered toward the corrals.

I drew a deep breath. Whatever Runnels had up
his sleeve, he had just carried it out. And he had
carried it out fast. I had to find out what they were
up to, but I couldn't figure out just how without
letting them know I had overheard their scheme.

His legs flopping up and down like a frightened
goose, Needle clung to the high-kicking pinto. He
was taking a beating. I would not have been surprised at all if his liver had plumb turned over from
the jostling he was taking.

That's when I knew how I could switch their attention from me long enough for me to slip into the
bunkhouse and see what kind of devious scheme
Runnels had had in mind.

While Needle caught his breath, I turned the pinto
into the broke corral and then from the trap corral
caught another horse to bust. It was a grulla—a
blue-gray, mousy-looking broomtail with black

points. After closing the gate, I forgot to slide the locking bar in place on purpose.

I led the grulla to my corral and locked the gate behind me. At that moment, a yell echoed from the trap corral, "The horses! They're loose!"

Everyone dropped what he was doing and raced for his own pony. I raced too, but for the bunkhouse. I only had seconds before someone realized I was not helping round up the horses. Since Runnels had only been out of my sight a few moments, I discounted the saddlebags. That would have taken time to unbuckle, then buckle.

My first guess was the mattress.

Inside, I yanked the mattress back. My eyes bulged. There, at the foot of the bed, lay a stack of greenbacks. Without hesitation, I grabbed them and jammed them under the mattress of Ike Bailey, one of Runnels's boys.

I ducked out a side window and raced for the trap corral. Just as I reached it, FW Red came around the corner of the barn pushing a couple horses ahead of him. I opened the gate, and when they raced inside, slammed it behind them. As the other ponies were herded back, I opened and closed the gate for them.

Once the horses were penned, Runnels demanded to know who had left the gate open. He glared at each of us. I spoke up. "Needle and me were in our corral saddling a grulla. I locked the gate behind me. Last one I saw at the corral was Carson."

Carson sputtered, "Not me. I locked the blasted gate."

I noticed that Needle arched a quizzical eyebrow at me, but he said nothing. I would explain later.

Runnels glared at me. I would have laid odds he figured I was lying, but he had no way to prove it. Even if he weren't certain, later tonight, when his little scheme backfired on him, he'd know for sure.

Chapter Six

After supper, FW Red, Needle, and me ambled out to the empty breaking corrals for a last smoke before turning in. Needle cleared his throat. "We hadn't even started to saddle that grulla this afternoon, Hobbs. Why did you tell Runnels we were?"

I cupped the match in my hands to light my cigarette. I offered the burning match to the others. While they dipped their heads toward my cupped hands, I explained, "For some reason, Runnels wants to run me off."

Needle drew back in surprise. "I don't believe that. You're too good a buster."

Glancing around to make sure no one would overhear me, I continued, "I already told FW Red, but remember when I went up on the rim to push strays down?"

"Yep. So?"

"So I saw Carson coming from the south where a bunch of buzzards were circling." I quickly detailed what I had discovered. "Then this afternoon when I was picking up a new rope from the tack room, I overheard Runnels tell Barton that dead hombre was a ranger."

Needle frowned. "A Texas Ranger?"

"That's what I'd guess."

"He went on to tell Barton he was going to run me off." I nodded to the bunkhouse. "He'll try tonight."

"How do you reckon he'll do that?" FW Red scratched at the three-day beard on his jaw.

I grinned. "Wait and see."

Needle shook his head. "I get the drift, but I reckon I don't see the whole picture. You think Carson killed the ranger?"

"Seems that way to me. Runnels complained that Carson didn't bury the ranger like Runnels had told him."

Shaking his head in wonder, FW Red said, "I never liked the jasper, but it's hard to believe he'd shoot down a Texas Ranger."

Keeping my eyes on the bunkhouse door in case Runnels or one of his boys came out, I replied, "Unless the ranger was on the trail of something Runnels didn't want discovered."

Needle tossed his cigarette to the ground and crushed it with his boot heel. "Like what?"

I shook my head. "I'm not sure. But I remember

something you said when we headed out for the south valleys the other day."

The lanky cowpoke frowned. "What was that?"

"You told me that you usually worked the same pastures and canyons for stock."

"That's right."

I looked at FW Red. "The other night, I ran into you up north. You always work that part of the ranch?"

"Yeah. Me and Needle."

"Coco and O.C.," Needle added.

"That means that Barton, Carson, and Bailey work the south sections of the ranch."

By now, dusk had given way to night, but even in the encroaching darkness, I could see the puzzlement on their faces.

"What are you driving at, Hobbs?" FW Red's frown deepened.

I remembered the worn trail leading to the rim. "To be truthful, I'm not sure. I've got an idea, but I'm not sure."

FW Red chuckled. "I think you're just letting your imagination run away with you. Runnels might be an unlikable hombre, but he's done Mister French a good job."

Needles nodded. "He has done that."

I didn't pursue the matter. I was more anxious to see the effect my switch would have on Runnels and his boys.

*   *   *

I didn't have long to wait. Ten minutes after we went back inside and got into a poker game, Runnels and Pete French, trailed by Little Pete and Miss Louisa, stormed into the bunkhouse.

"Boys," Runnels growled. "Someone has stolen a heap of greenbacks from Mister French's desk." He looked at me, a sneer on his grizzled face. Then he spoke to all of us again. "If any of you took it, give it back and I'll let you ride out. If you don't, we'll tear this bunkhouse apart. When we find it, I'll stomp the thief into a mudhole."

Miss Louisa and Little Pete stood in the open doorway, eyes wide.

I glanced at Barton. He wore a smug look on his face.

Clearing my throat, I stepped forward. "Seeing as I'm the newest hand, Mister French, I couldn't blame you if you wanted to search my plunder first."

My volunteering wiped the self-satisfied grin from Runnels's face for a moment. The old man hesitated, but Runnels grunted. "I reckon we might as well. We never had no trouble around here until you came along, Hobbs."

With a big grin, I gestured to my bunk. "Go right ahead."

With a flourish, Runnels grabbed the mattress and yanked it up. "Just what I—" His words clogged in his throat and his eyes bugged out like a stepped-on toad frog when he saw the greenbacks were missing.

"Here," I said, reaching under the bunk to retrieve

my saddlebags. "Look in here while you're at it, Runnels." Before he could respond, I dumped the contents of the bags on the mattress.

"All I have is my six-gun and belt, a second six-gun, an extra shirt, some Bull Durham, cartridges, and a deerskin jacket," I added, holding the fringed jacket up for everyone to see.

Runnels glowered at Barton, who tried to suppress the sudden expression of consternation on his face. Runnels then looked at me. When he spotted the faint grin on my face, his eyes grew hard. Keeping his eyes on me, he growled, "Don't look like it's Hobbs, Mister French."

A look of relief washed the frown from the old man's face. He nodded and grinned. "That's good, Hobbs."

"Thanks." I turned to Runnels, then gestured to the rest of the bunkhouse. "I reckon you'd better get on with your search, Mister Runnels."

He glowered at me. I knew Runnels was wondering just how in the Sam Hill his plan had gone wrong. I didn't laugh at his confusion, but the smug grin on my face told him exactly who had outsmarted him.

Ten minutes later, Runnels jerked Ike Bailey's mattress back and a stack of greenbacks stared him in the face.

Bailey's jaw dropped open. He turned to the old man. "Mister French. I—I didn't put the money there. I don't know anything about it, honest. I—"

A round of muttered threats came from the other cowpokes, drowning out his protest.

French barked at the surprised cowboy, "You're fired, Bailey. Pack your gear and get out, now. I'll give orders to have you shot on sight if you show your thieving face around here again." He picked up his money.

As Pete French counted his money, Runnels turned and stared at me. I gave him a brief nod, answering the question in his mind. He clenched his jaw. My grin grew broader.

"Help me, Runnels." The expression in Bailey's eyes pleaded for help from the range boss.

Runnels shook his head. "You heard Mister French. Pack up and get out." He cut his eyes back to me, and from the fury boiling in them, I knew I had an enemy for life.

After Bailey pulled foot and Runnels went back to the house with the old man, the rest of us, with the exception of Barton and Carson, sat around discussing the surprising events of the evening. To a man, each was surprised. While Ike Bailey had not been close to anyone except Carson and Barton, he was one of the ranch hands, which meant he was trusted by all.

"Makes a man wonder," O.C. muttered. "Things getting so bad that one of these days, we'll have to take to locking the front door, I reckon."

"Naw," drawled Needle. "It'll never come to that. He just happened to be the rotten apple."

I glanced at Barton and Carson. Their heads were together, and they were whispering. From time to time, one would glance in my direction. I just gave them a sympathetic shake of my head.

Rolling a cigarette, I went outside for some fresh air. FW Red followed me. "Is that what you meant earlier?"

"Yep."

He studied me a moment. "You think Runnels wanted you to get the blame for stealing the money." It was not a question, but an observation.

"Yep."

He nodded slowly, beginning to understand what had taken place. "So Bailey didn't really steal the money?"

"Nope."

"Then how did it get in his bunk?"

I chuckled. "I put it there."

His eyes grew wide. "You did what?"

"I put it there. I spotted Runnels slipping into the bunkhouse this afternoon. He put the money under my mattress. Runnels figured I'd get run off. Instead, it was his pal, Bailey, who was run off. Remember when the horses got loose?"

"Yeah."

"That was me. While you old boys was out rounding them up, I sneaked into the bunkhouse and switched the money to Bailey's bunk." I shrugged. "I hated to put the blame on someone like that, but he was in thick with Runnels in whatever they're up to."

"But you was at the gate when I brought the horses back."

"I had just got back to the gate."

FW Red blew softly through his lips. "Hold on, Pardner. Things are moving a mite too fast for me, but if what you say is right, and since Runnels missed this chance to run you off, then that means—"

I finished his observation for him. "That means he'll try something else."

"So what are you going to do?"

"That, my friend, I don't know. But believe me, I'll figure something out."

Later, Runnels stomped back into the bunkhouse, and without a word, stalked to his bunk. He paused at Carson's bunk, muttering to the prone man. He was referring to me because Carson inadvertently cut his eyes in my direction.

At the present, I had Runnels off balance. But it has often been my experience that just about when you think you've got a bear on the run, he'll turn and tear your head off with one of his paws.

O.C. shuffled over to the lantern in his bare feet. "Here goes the light, boys," he announced, lifting the chimney and blowing out the flame.

I lay awake for several minutes, trying to plan my next step, but I was at a disadvantage because I didn't know what form of payback Runnels had in mind.

Chapter Seven

T he excited chatter around the breakfast table the next morning still centered on Ike Bailey. It shut down instantly as soon as Runnels, followed by Carson and Barton, entered. They served up their grub in tin plates and sat at the far end of the table.

He growled at us, "Hurry up, Boys. We want to finish the horses today. Push them on up to Camp Verde." He fixed his black eyes on mine. "We can't afford no mistakes."

I read the intent in his words. What he meant was that *he* could not afford any more mistakes.

So we hurried. By six A.M. dust was boiling up in the corral, wild ponies were squealing, and cowboys were shouting and cursing.

Mid-morning, Miss Louisa and Little Pete came to watch.

Needle and me stayed busy. About the only time either had for conversation was when the other was in saddle, getting his insides turned upside down.

That's when Miss Louisa sidled up to me, her eyes still on the dun Needle was forking. "I'm sorry about last night."

I frowned at her. "Last night?"

She looked up, her eyebrows knit in worry. "When they searched your bunk. I knew you couldn't have stole Pa's money."

With a soft chuckle, I shrugged. "Don't worry none on my part. They were searching everyone. They didn't have anyone singled out."

She smiled gratefully. "I just didn't want you to feel like we didn't trust you."

I paused before climbing through the rails. "Don't fret, Miss Louisa. I don't feel that way."

While I was taking the dun back to the broke pen, Little Pete fell in by my side. "You think you can still show me about busting horses tomorrow, Lew?"

"Don't know why not," I replied, grinning down at the youngster.

By the time I returned, Needle had us a wild-eyed roan that acted like he wanted nothing more than to stomp us into the ground. We tied him up short to the snubbing post, but he had another trick in his catalog. Each time we approached with the saddle, he bolted sideways just far enough to get out from under the saddle.

Needle let loose with a string of profanity, some words I'd never heard even in all my traveling.

But I decided the red-speckled roan was playing games with us. In fact, I halfway admired the spunky animal's determination not to go under the saddle. "Go ahead and play your tricks, Fella. I've fooled with enough like you to know how to stop them." I swung out a loop and tossed the rope over his neck so the loop dropped to the ground. He twitched his neck and shook his head, but remained motionless until I took a step toward him.

He stepped away from me, right into the loop on the ground, which I quickly tightened and jerked his front leg up to his chest. I handed the other end to Needle. "Hold him tight. He won't go anywhere on three feet."

The roan tried to reach back and bite me, but he was tied up tighter than a fly in a spiderweb. "Sorry, Old Boy. That's the breaks." I saddled him, and as I was tightening the cinch, I spotted Runnels riding out, heading south.

I couldn't help wondering if he was going to meet Ike Bailey.

I didn't see him ride back in, but he was at the supper table that night.

I realized when I woke up the next morning that the day was Sunday, not only the day I had promised Little Pete a few lessons on a bucking calf, but also the day the boys claimed I would or would not get my invite to Sunday dinner. I was as jittery as a mail-order bride.

At breakfast, Runnels threw water on my expectations for the day when he gave FW Red, Needle, and me the job of pushing thirty head up to Camp Verde. I shook my head, realizing that both that both my lesson with the youngster and the dinner invitation was going to be cancelled.

"Today?" I sipped my coffee.

Runnels shook his head. "Tomorrow. Mister French don't believe in doing more than looking after stock on Sundays unless something turns up mighty pressing."

I grinned. My hopes surged, and I looked forward to dinner with the Frenches as well as spending some time with Little Pete. I looked up from my plate of eggs and steak. "You done this before? I mean, pushed a herd to Camp Verde?" I asked of FW Red.

"You bet. It's an easy ride. Three days up there and back. That's even counting a few hours at the tables and with the ladies at the Red Dog Saloon."

Needle nodded emphatically. "That's my favorite part of the whole blasted trip," he said with a grin.

Chapter Eight

Little Pete was waiting outside the chuck house the next morning when I emerged from a hearty breakfast. He looked at me hopefully, his freckled face animated with excitement. "Are you ready, Lew? Huh? Huh?"

When I spotted him, I hoped he was bearing the dinner invitation, but I hid my disappointment. Before I could reply, an angry voice called out from around the corner, "Peter John, you get back here, right now!" I looked around just as Miss Louisa, dressed in her Sunday best, rushed around the corner, brows knit, obviously put out with her little brother. "I'll twist you ear off, you little scamp. I'll—oh!" She jerked to a halt in surprise when she saw me. Her dark-complexioned cheeks grew darker. "I—I'm sorry. I didn't see you." She looked

past me at her brother. She jabbed a finger at him.
"I was looking for him."

I nodded. "Morning. Right pretty day."

Momentarily confused, she agreed. "Yes. Yes it
is." She smiled up at me. Abruptly, she turned back
to her brother. Her smile vanished. "We'll be late.
Come along, Peter John. We're leaving for church."

The young boy took a step backward and shook
his head. "I ain't going. Lew is going to teach me
to bust calves. Honest."

I spoke up. "Hold on, Sprout. Your pa's got to
okay it first."

"Oh, he will, he will. Honest."

"He won't do any such thing, Peter John, especially if you make him late for church. Now you
come on, you hear?" She glanced up at me, lowered
her eyes demurely, and gave a slight curtsy. "Nice
to see you, Mister Hobbs. You're more than welcome to attend services with us."

"Thank you, Miss. I reckon I'll hang around and
tend my pony. Old Bill has been feeling somewhat
neglected."

"I understand," she said. "But you are welcome."
She shot her brother a warning look. Her voice grew
brittle. "Let's go, Peter John."

Little Pete shook his head. "No." He looked up
at me hopefully. "I don't mind staying and helping
you tend Bill, Lew. Honest."

I chuckled. "No. You get along with your sister.
We'll talk this afternoon."

A frown wrinkled his forehead. "Aww."

"Nope." I shook my head. "You want me to show you about riding calves, you get on to church with your sister before your pa comes after you."

"Aww." He shook his head and kicked at the hardpan with the toe of his boot. "That ain't fair."

I suppressed a grin. "No one said it was, Boy. Now git. Come see me when you get back."

Miss Louisa gave me an appreciative smile that was very becoming, but she didn't say a word about dinner. I tried to tell myself to forget about it. No one wanted a drifter like me for part of the family. But a tiny flame of hope still flickered in the back of my head.

After dinner, Needle and FW Red ambled up under the shady oak where I was grooming Bill. Needle was whittling away on a chunk of pine, and FW Red was coiling and uncoiling a short rope. They were restless. Cowboys don't have much spare time, and when they do, they're often hard put to figure out how to use it. That's why they usually end up in some kind of trouble, whether it's for shooting holes in the saloon ceiling or trying to steal a kiss from a saloon girl.

"Fine-looking animal," Needle drawled, not taking his eyes off his whittling.

"What are you making?" I asked, keeping my eyes on Bill's mane as I brushed the tangles from it.

"Toothpick," he replied in all seriousness.

I glanced at the chunk of wood. It was a foot long and three inches wide. "Looks like an all-day job to me."

He nodded. "That's about what I figured. Got a day off so to speak, reckon I ought to do something productive."

"Seems that way," I muttered.

Even the Sunday conversation seemed to be drifting about, restless-like.

"Got the invite yet?" Needle drawled.

"Nope."

He clucked his tongue and shook his head.

FW Red built a small loop about twelve inches across and spun it up and down and sideways. While paying attention to his twirling rope, he said, "How come you don't wear a side gun, Hobbs? You got one. I saw it when you dumped your plunder on the bunk the other night." He paused, then added, " 'Course, if you figure it ain't none of my business, just say so. I ain't sensitive to put-downs. I might cry a little at night about it, but I'll be right perky in the morning."

I couldn't resist grinning. "All I know is that when you wear one, sometimes you use it when you shouldn't. The better you are, the more those times seem to crop up."

His eyes on his whittling, Needle drawled, "You that good?"

Without looking at him, I replied, "Nobody's that good."

"Well, I tell you, Pardner. If you handle that six-gun the way you handled that Winchester back at the canyon with them two Comanches, you might be that nobody."

With a grunt, I replied, "Told you, luck. Every once in a while, I get lucky."

To my relief, FW Red changed the subject. "Well, I hope I'm lucky when we hit the Red Dog Saloon in Camp Verde. I got me a few dollars I want to try on faro."

Needle nodded. "Me too."

He was still whittling on his toothpick when Little Pete returned, all set to learn the art of bronc busting. He patted his stomach. "I didn't mean to be late, Lew, but Ma wouldn't let me leave until I finished Sunday dinner."

I felt like an angry bronc had kicked me in the belly. While I had continually reminded myself I would not be invited to dinner, I was still disappointed. I forced a grin for the excited boy. "That's all right, Little Pete." I took a deep breath and told myself it was for the best. No sense in raising hopes too high. After all, the bigger the horse, the farther a jasper has to fall. "Let's get to your first lesson."

First, I explained that he was too small for a full-sized bronc, but he could learn some of the basics on calves. And that's where we started, on jumpy, jittery, half-grown calves. Earlier, after I finished grooming Bill, I had rigged a hackamore to fit a calf, so we had all the equipment we needed.

We spent the afternoon in the barn corral, where Little Pete spent more time in the air and on the ground than he did on the back of those frisky little calves. From time to time, without thinking, I glanced at the main house. When I realized what I was doing, I jerked my attention back to Little Pete, at the same time chiding myself for acting like a lovestruck youngster.

Since not much was taking place around the ranch on a Sunday afternoon, the hands drifted over to the corral for some entertainment, and before long, the young buster-to-be had more advice than he could handle.

Now, even if a body has never been in a cow lot, he would instantly recognize the wisdom of carefully picking his way through the cow patties. But when you're flying through the air like Little Pete was, you can't pick your landing spots.

He had flattened about three-fourths of those cow patties when he decided to call it quits. As he slowly climbed to his feet, O.C. called out, "Don't stop now, Little Pete. There's still a few cow patties you ain't mashed down."

We laughed at the boy's expense, but when I nodded to him and told him he'd done a fine job for a beginner, the grimace on his face turned into a bright smile. "You really mean that, Lew? Honest?"

Careful of where I laid my hand on his shoulder,

I grinned back. "You bet, Buster. You're a fast learner." I winked at Miss Louisa who was riding the opera rail, then gently nudged Little Pete to the gate. "Now, you best get cleaned up. You done enough work for today."

Miss Louisa came over to us, a bright smile on her face. She wrinkled her nose when she stopped next to her little brother. "You best not go in the house with those clothes on. Your sister is already sick. She smells all that, she'll even be sicker."

Suddenly, my once dead dreams came back to life. "Miss Alicia's sick?"

Miss Louisa rolled her eyes. "She's always sick. I think she did it today just so she wouldn't have to go to church like the rest of us."

I just nodded, tickled to realize that maybe her illness was the reason I hadn't gotten a dinner invitation.

Throughout the day, Runnels and his boys were nowhere to be seen. Just before sunset, they came riding in from the south. I gazed beyond them, remembering the dead ranger I had run across earlier. The hair on the back of my neck bristled. Runnels was up to something, but what?

Carson and Barton rode to the barn while Runnels stopped at the main house. At about that time, our cook rang the bell, and we all scooted toward the chuck house.

We were all busy shoveling fried steak, gravy, and biscuits down our gullets when Runnels stomped in. He paused in the open door and stared at me, a sneer on his lips. "Eat up, you three. You push out tomorrow early for Camp Verde." He paused and added, "Take care. Don't want nothing to happen to you or them soldier-boys' horses." From the emphasis he put on his words, I knew he wasn't talking about the horses.

"Don't worry, Runnels," I replied, a hint of sarcasm in my tone. "We'll make sure nothing happens to the horses."

"Or us," FW Red put in, completely oblivious to the undertones in the conversation between Runnels and me.

Runnels's sneer grew wider. "We'll see. Move out early. With luck, you should reach Antelope Springs by nightfall."

I glanced at Needle and FW Red. Neither cowpoke seemed to sense the animosity in the range boss's tone.

That night as Needle removed his boots, he spoke to FW Red. "You bring Sally in?"

"Yep. In the corral."

I glanced at Needle. He saw the question on my face. "Our bell mare," he said. "Old Sally, a chestnut. I reckon she knows the trail to Camp Verde better than us."

We rode out before the sun next morning, Needle at point ahead of Old Sally, FW Red at flank, and me, since I was the new wrangler on the spread, riding drag, eating the dust. The day was cloudy, threatening rain from the southwest.

We caught our first shower in mid-afternoon and spent the remainder of the day dodging the rain while maintaining a steady gait through the rugged country of limestone boulders and stunted cedar. We camped at Antelope Springs that night. According to FW Red, we'd covered about forty miles. Another twenty or so to Camp Verde, which meant we'd arrive some time after noon the next day.

Off to the west was a rocky bluff extending north before curving back to the west. To the east lay a grassy meadow where the horses could graze until morning.

During FW Red's watch, another light shower passed over, taking with it the clouds and leaving a fresh-washed sky filled with millions of sparkling stars.

Though the soft tinkling of Old Sally's bell reassured us that the ponies were fine, we took turns on watch. When Needle relieved me, he shivered. "Chilly out here tonight," he muttered. "Reckon it was the rain."

I laughed and fished my deerskin jacket from my saddlebags. "Here, wear this." I tossed it to him.

"Obliged, Hobbs. Obliged."

The next morning dawned bright and clear. The cool air was crisp, and the song of the birds seemed to have an extra clarity.

I had just squatted when the coffeepot exploded. Then I head the boom of a rifle. In the same instant, I threw myself backwards over an old log on which I had placed my saddle.

A barrage of gunfire tore up the camp. FW Red shouted, "What the blazes is going on?"

"Stay down," I shouted, popping up long enough to yank my Winchester from my saddle and then hunker back down against the log. I felt the impact of the slugs slamming into the log and my saddle.

From the herd came the jangling of the bell, not the gentle tinkling of a grazing animal, but the clanging of running horses. Mixed with the clamor of the bell were the distant shouts of the rustlers driving the herd away. The gunfire pinning us down continued.

Just as suddenly as the gunfire began, it ceased. The silence that fell over the camp was even more pronounced because of the racketing fusillade of just a few moments earlier.

In the distance, the hoofbeats of the herd slowly died away.

Taking my time, I peered over the seat of the saddle, only to jerk back down as a single shot slammed into the campfire.

"Hobbs! You okay?" It was FW Red.

"Yeah. What about Needle?"

FW Red called his name. No answer. "Maybe they're gone."

"Don't take a chance," I shouted back. "They're up on the rim."

Another shot rang out. I looked around, searching for a spot where I could at least get off a shot or two. Other than the log, there was no cover for twenty feet. I'd be lucky if I made five of them before I'd catch a lead plum in my back. So, I just lay where I was.

Then I heard a groan.

"FW Red! You hit?"

"Not me. I'm behind a big slab of rock. You?"

"No. Must be Needle. You see him?"

"Not from here. Needle! You hurt?"

Our only answer was another groan.

"Let me scoot down some." Anxiously I waited, and then FW Red called out, "I see him. He's out in the open. He's been hit in the back."

I thought fast. "Is he closer to you or me?"

"Me!"

"All right then. Here's what we'll do. The shots are coming from the canyon rim. I'll jump up and try to keep them penned down while you haul him back behind your rock."

For a long moment, FW Red didn't reply.

"You hear me?"

There wasn't a heap of enthusiasm in his voice when he replied. "Yeah. I hear you."

"All right. Tell me when you're ready."

Several silent seconds passed. "FW Red? You hear me?"

"Yeah. Yeah, I hear you."

"Well? Whenever you're ready."

"I ain't ready. Not yet."

"Why not?"

"Those jaspers, they're shooting real bullets."

I couldn't help grinning. No hombre, at least, no smart hombre, likes to jump deliberately into harm's way. Before I could reply, Needle groaned again.

His friend's groans galvanized FW Red into action. He shouted, "What the blazes! Let's go right now."

I leaped to my feet, clanking one cartridge after another into the chamber and squeezing off shots at the rim above, trying to pace the slugs so FW Red would have time to grab Needle and haul him back behind the slab. One by one, I counted the number of cartridges. I had fifteen to work with.

Straggly sage dotted the rim, providing a blind behind which I figured the bushwhackers hid. I did my best to blast the small shrubs loose from the thin soil to which the roots clung among the rocks.

I still had three cartridges in the magazine when FW Red heaved Needle behind the rock slab. I dropped to the ground next to the log and quickly reloaded, expecting return fire, but a strange silence settled over the camp as the echoes of my gunfire died away.

"How is he?" I called out.

FW Red's voice broke. "Not—not good, Hobbs. I think he's dying. I think Old Needle is dying."

Chapter Nine

"Keep your head down," I called out. Using caution, I peered above the saddle, then jerked my head back down.

Nothing.

"Listen. When I tell you, shoot at the rim. I'll try to get to you."

"Yeah. Okay."

I bunched my legs, then shouted, "Now!"

He pumped off six fast shots. I don't know if they hit the rim or not, but no one took a potshot at me as I sprinted the thirty feet to the limestone slab. From that, I reckoned they had hightailed it after their compadres.

FW Red looked at me, tears in his eyes. "Hobbs, see what you can do. Old Needle sure looks like he's going to pack it in."

I knelt by the wheezing man. Bright red blood gathered at the sides of his lips. I opened his shirt and saw the same bright red blood bubbling from the hole in his chest and darker blood from the one in his belly. I closed my eyes and shook my head.

"What do you think? Can't we just plug him up?"

Without taking my eyes from Needle, I replied, "Lung-shot and belly-shot. We need to make him as comfortable as we can."

"We got to get him to the doctor in Camp Verde." FW Red looked around and cursed. "They even took our ponies. Now what?"

Rising, I looked at FW Red. "He's got no chance, FW Red. That's why I say make him comfortable."

Tears cut streaks in the smaller man's grimy cheeks and dripped from his jaw. He dropped to his knees by the wheezing cowpoke. "Lord, Needle. I never reckoned it would be you first. I always figured since I was the wild one, I'd head up to the Great Divide ahead of you."

Needle's eyes cracked open. A faint grin twitched over his lips. "I-I ain't too fond of making this trip myself," he whispered, breaking into a frail laugh at his joke despite his wounds. He grimaced as a series of hacking coughs seized him.

FW Red laid his hand on Needle's shoulder. "Easy, Pard. Easy. Don't talk. We're going to bandage you up and get you to the doc. You'll be just fine. And then we're going to have one whale of a time at the Red Dog Saloon in Camp Verde." Tears dripped on his dusty sleeves.

Needle dragged the tip of his tongue over his parched lips. His voice was a mere whisper. "Afraid—afraid I ain't going to make that trip. But we seen and done a heap together. I ain't complaining."

FW Red dragged a dusty sleeve across his eyes. "Me neither. I—I—ah—" His words caught in his throat. He squeezed Needle's thin hands in his own.

Needles looked up at him, and even as we watched, the glaze of death slid over his eyes, a dull film covering the shiny glitter of life.

"Needle?" FW Red squeezed his friend's hand. "Needle!" His voice grew louder, then almost strident. "Needle! Listen to me!"

"He can't," I whispered.

FW Red broke down and cried like a baby.

We dug a shallow grave on the edge of the meadow. Just before we lowered Needle into it, FW Red said, "Ain't that your jacket he's wearing?"

"He was cold last night. Maybe it will keep him warm on his trip now." We covered the shallow grave with rocks. FW Red worked silently, stoically.

When we finished, we spent a few minutes in silence, studying the grave. Finally, FW Red turned and cleared his throat. In a gruff voice, he said,

"Well, now I reckon we'd best head on to Camp Verde. We got a good piece to walk."

"Not so far," I replied, nodding back to the camp.

Bill stood beside the saddle, watching us.

"But I thought the rustlers took him along with the others."

I chuckled and whistled. Bill trotted to us. He nuzzled up to me, and I scratched his head behind his ear, his favorite scratching spot. "That's what make this old boy so special. He'll always come back given any chance at all."

With a frown, FW Red shook his head. "How'd you teach him to do that?"

I held Bill's head over my shoulder, scratching behind both ears. "Beats me. Seems like I always had a kinship with animals, horses especially. Isn't that right, Old Boy?"

Bill nickered and nodded his head two or three times.

We rode double into Camp Verde. During the ride, I had time to think, to filter through a few ideas that had been tumbling about in my head.

I couldn't shake the idea that for whatever reason, Bart Runnels was behind the bushwhacking and rustling. Maybe he had sold the Army the horses himself. After all, they would bring about eighteen hundred dollars, over four years' wages for a cowpoke.

But my little theory blew up in my face like gunpowder when we reached Camp Verde and learned no horses had been brought in.

"I'm mighty sorry to hear about your troubles, Mister Hobbs," said the lieutenant at the post. "But I'm even more sorry that we didn't get the horses. We're remount shy. Those animals would have come in right handy."

FW Red and I exchanged looks. "Maybe next time we'll get them in here, Lieutenant."

After Needle, neither of us had any inclination to chase the tiger over at the Red Dog Saloon that night. Instead, we camped outside of town and pushed out early next morning for the Bar F.

We rode in silence for the first hour, then FW Red glanced at me. "Did you get any kind of look at the rustlers, Hobbs?"

"Nope. Not hide nor hair."

"Think it was Comanches?"

I shrugged. "I've been considering it. Stands to reason that white men would have likely sold them to the Army, then pull foot out of the country. Comanches, well, who knows about them. On the other hand, the Goodnight-Loving Trail is a couple days north and the Chisholm east. The rustlers might have figured we would check with the army at Camp Verde, so they pushed on up, planning to sell the horses to one of the drives heading for Wichita or Dodge."

We reached Antelope Springs in mid-afternoon.

FW Red reined his pony toward the pasture. "I'd like to see Needle."

I pointed to the rim from which our ambushers had fired. "While you do, I'm going to take a look up there. Maybe they left something that'll give us an idea who they were."

FW Red snorted and shook his head. "Not likely."

He was just about right except for the cigarette paper I found caught in the tangled branches of a berry briar. Figuring it to be mighty unlikely that Comanches had started rolling their own cigarettes, I guessed maybe it had been whites who had ambushed us.

I continued searching. Whoever had been up here had been mighty careful. They had picked up their empty cartridges, but then I got lucky. I found a .44 caliber cartridge with an H on the rim, a mark on all cartridges manufactured for a Henry.

For several seconds, I studied the empty hull, remembering the Yellowboy Henry I had seen booted on Joe Carson's rig. I slipped it in my vest pocket along with the cigarette paper.

Before returning to the valley below, I studied the tracks in the soil, which, despite the rain, was too sandy to hold any impressions that would help identify the bushwhackers. All I had was the paper and empty cartridge, and a few ideas tumbling around in that empty skull of mine.

We rode another twenty miles before making camp in a hollow back under a rocky bluff. We shielded the fire from outside, then extinguished it after supper.

Though neither of us was sleepy, we weren't in the mood to talk. We lay silently, each with his own thoughts. I weighed and sifted through all that had happened, even to me loaning Needle the use of my deerskin jacket.

Next morning as we squatted around the small fire, sipping coffee and chewing on jerky, FW Red fixed his eyes on me. "I've been thinking, Hobbs. I ain't got no proof, but I'd wager my last dollar that it wasn't Comanches that killed Needle and stole Pete's horses."

Remembering the cigarette paper and the empty casing I'd found on the rim, I said, "What makes you think that?"

He held the hot coffee mug in his cupped hands. He shook his head. "Hard to say, exactly. Except, maybe because the raid was too smooth, too planned. I've fought my share of Indians, and from what I've seen, Comanches usually come in hollering and screaming, not all quiet like that bunch day before yesterday."

Had he not broached the subject, I probably would never have brought him into my confidence, for a lack of interest never gets the cows milked.

But his observation told me he was willing to milk the cows. I fished the cigarette paper from my vest pocket. "I agree," I said, holding the paper for him to see.

With a frown, he said, "What's that?"

"What it looks like. I found it on the rim yesterday while you were at Needle's grave."

He studied the paper a moment, skepticism obvious in his eyes. "No telling how long it was up there."

"Look at it. It's dry."

FW Red frowned.

I explained. "You've rolled enough cigarettes to know what happens to paper if it's too wet."

"Reckon so. It falls apart." Suddenly, his eyes lit up in understanding. "I see what you're saying. It had been raining the night before. In fact, the last rain started when I went out for my watch."

"That's right," I replied, folding the cigarette paper back into my vest pocket. "Whoever dropped the paper dropped it after the rain. And last I noticed, Comanches don't roll cigarettes."

FW Red set his jaw. His eyes grew cold. "They didn't just stumble across us, did they?"

"Not likely. I think someone planned it, the same someone who killed that ranger back south of the Bar F." I hesitated, wondering if I should say more. I decided to gamble, banking on the fact Needle and FW Red had been longtime compadres. "The fact that Needle was wearing my jacket convinces me who's behind it all."

"The jacket?"

I nodded slowly, fixing my eyes on his. "I believe whoever shot Needle thought he was shooting me."

FW Red gaped at me in surprise. "You?"

"Stop and think about it. Runnels tried to frame me for stealing Pete's money. Why? Because Carson saw me coming down from the rim after he had killed that ranger."

Frowning, the smaller man shoved his hat to the back of his head and studied me. "Runnels, huh?" He shook his head. "I don't cotton to the man, but I never figured him for a thief."

"Or killer," I added.

FW Red's eyes grew cold.

"Tell me," I said, retrieving the empty casing from my vest pocket. "I know Carson carries a Henry. What about Runnels and Barton?"

A puzzled looked crossed his face. "Yeah, Barton does. Why?"

I handed him the shell. "This was on the rim also."

He turned it over in his hand. "How do you know it's a Henry?"

I explained the H on the rim.

FW Red pursed his lips and cursed softly. "Those no good, dirty . . ."

Chapter Ten

W e rode out after breakfast, still discussing my theory. The country was growing rougher the closer we drew to Frio Canyon.

Finally, we dropped down into the canyon. I said, "I know Runnels came in and cut back on the rustling, but what if he was the one doing the rustling to begin with? What if he decided he could make more by stealing a few head every week or month instead of one big raid?"

"Where would he keep them? Not on the Bar F."

"Didn't you say that usually Runnels or his men work the south range?"

"Yep, but not all the time. All of us work it from time to time."

A grin sprang to my lips. "When he isn't moving stock."

FW Red shook his head. "I don't follow."

"When Needle and me worked the south end, I rode up to the rim to bring down any cows up there. The trail had been used a heap. They could push cows up to the rim, then hide them in a box canyon somewhere until they had enough to sell to passing cattle drives. Then, ever so often, he sends other ranch hands to work the range. Naturally, everything looks fine to them, but when his boys get back, they move a few more head."

FW Red blew through his lips. "Not a bad idea. I—"

Before he could say another word, the blood-curdling roar of a bear and a single gunshot rolled out of an offshoot canyon to our right. We reined up and looked at each other.

"What do you think?" FW Red muttered, nervously studying the canyon entrance.

Another guttural growl echoed from the canyon, sending chills down my spine and raising goose bumps on my arms. I shucked my saddle gun. "I don't know. Sounds like some poor jasper has done gone and upset himself a bear." I touched my heels to the dun's flanks, and we headed into the canyon.

"Go easy," FW Red cautioned.

That was one warning he did not have to give. While the grizzly and black bear populations were not as they had been a hundred years earlier, there were enough of them around to make an hombre mighty cautious.

And careful was what I was as I headed back into the canyon from which a narrow stream flowed into confluence with the Rio Frio. Bill's ears were perked forward. I could feel his muscles tense through my legs. "Easy, Boy," I whispered. "Easy."

The canyon was maybe a hundred yards wide, not nearly as wide as I would have preferred going up against a thousand-pound creature armed with crushing jaws and razor claws and speed matching that of a horse over a short burst.

The growling ceased, but from deeper in the canyon came the sounds of snapping limbs.

"There!" FW Red shouted. "The edge of the clearing."

Across the clearing, a bear stood on its hind legs trying to slap an Indian warrior from the overhead branches. A sense of relief washed over me. The good news was that it was a black bear, not a grizzly, but the bad news was that black bears climb trees with unmatched agility.

And at that moment, the bear decided to put on a show. She started up the trunk of the tall pecan tree, and when she did, the Indian scampered ten feet higher. He was looking around desperately, searching for a nearby tree to which he might possibly leap. There were none.

I squeezed my legs, pushing Bill forward, at the same time throwing the Winchester into my shoulder and squeezing off a shot above the bear. The slug tore a chunk from the trunk of the pecan.

She ignored the warning. I fired again, hoping to spook the savage beast from the tree. The second shot worked. The bear looked around, then dropped, bounced off a limb, and slammed to the ground.

Instantly, she was on her feet and charging us, jaws agape, her deadly teeth gleaming white.

FW Red and I split up, and the bear took after FW Red. I slid the Winchester back in the boot and grabbed my reata, quickly building a loop and racing after the bear.

Leaning low over his horse's neck, FW Red urged his sorrel into a wide circle through the canyon, dodging trees and splashing through the small stream with the black bear right behind him, growling and roaring in anger and rage.

I leaned forward and squeezed my legs hard, forcing Bill into a gallop. "Get me close, Boy. Get me close." I kept waiting for the bear to spot me, but her fury focused all her attention on FW Red and his pony.

I'd roped many hind feet of running horses and cows. I figured a bear wasn't a whole lot different. At twenty feet, I tossed an underhand loop, sort of a modified hoolihan, at the hind legs of the bear. The loop settled under the hind right foot of the black bear. I dallied the end of the rope around the saddle horn and yanked Bill into a sharp right.

The rope tightened and jerked the bear's leg from under her, sending her slamming to the ground, but only for an instant. Immediately, she leaped to her feet and charged me. I sent Bill racing toward the stream, then cut back to the right again.

Before the bear could make her move to follow, FW Red's loop settled over her head, popping her to the ground. We backed away from her, keeping our ropes taut and her on the ground, bawling and growling.

"Now what?" FW Red shouted.

I shook my head and dragged the back of my arm across my sweaty forehead. "Loosen up a bit. Let her get to her feet. See if she's learned her lesson."

"What if she ain't?"

"Then we'll bust her again."

As soon as she felt slack, she charged me. We busted her again.

This time, when she climbed to her feet, she had learned her lesson. Instead of charging one of us, she stood motionless for a few seconds, then turned toward the mouth of the canyon.

We dropped our ropes, and she dragged them after her, shaking her head and foot as she walked, loosening the loops until she shook them off.

We turned back to the Indian up in the pecan tree, at the same time keeping a wary eye on the retreating bear.

With one arm, the brave clung to a limb high in the tree, as frightened of us as he had been of the bear. Blood ran down his other arm, already forming a pool on the ground beneath him.

I made the southern tribes' sign for friend, hooking my index fingers together in front of my chest. I held up my canteen and motioned him down.

He cut his eyes toward FW Red, then back to me. Once again, I gestured for him to descend. Reluctantly, he started down, one limb at a time. Once or twice, he hesitated and closed his eyes. I held my breath, hoping he had not lost so much blood that he would pass out. He was still twenty feet up, and such a fall could possibly kill him.

When he reached the ground, he put out his hand against the trunk of the tree to steady himself. From his complexion, I couldn't tell if his face was pale or not, but I had my answer when his eyes rolled up in his head, and he collapsed.

I dismounted quickly, but FW Red stayed in the saddle. As I knelt by the Indian, FW Red grunted. "What the Sam Hill you taking care of him for? He's a savage. He'd just as soon cut your throat as look at you."

Without looking around at him, I replied. "I'd do the same for you."

He said nothing, just watched silently as I tipped the canteen to the unconscious Indian's lips. The wiry brave coughed, then shuddered and opened his eyes, which grew wide in alarm when they saw me. I made the sign for friend once again. He relaxed. I offered him the canteen. He drank greedily.

His arm was bleeding profusely. I examined the deep cuts. They needed stitches, which was impossible out here in the middle of the wilderness. I pulled out an old shirt and tore it up for bandages. "This is the best I can do," I told him as I wrapped his arm tightly, staunching most of the blood flow. "I don't reckon you can understand me, but this ought to slow the bleeding down enough so the blood will clot." I helped him to his feet and nodded to his arm. "You should be fine until you can get back to your people."

He nodded slowly, and to my surprise, said, "You help Run With Horse. I not forget."

Behind me, FW Red swore. "Well, I'll be switched. That Injun can talk 'Merican almost good as me. Ain't that a kicker?"

I glanced around, looking for Run With Horse's pony. I gestured down the valley. "Horse." I pointed at his chest. "Your horse?"

He nodded in the direction I pointed. "There." He cupped his hand to his mouth and gave a series of loud chirps. Within seconds, his pinto pony emerged from the trees and trotted to us.

FW Red whistled. "That's some trick."

"You be all right?" I asked of Run With Horse.

Blood still dripped from the tips of his fingers. "I go to my people."

He was weaker than pond water, for I had to help him climb on his pony. He struggled to sit upright. He looked at me, then started his pony toward the mouth of the canyon.

We watched as he disappeared. FW Red shook his head. "Never thought I'd see that."

"What?"

"A Comanche and a white man that close together without fighting."

I climbed into the saddle and laughed. "Maybe some of us don't like to fight."

He chuckled. "Tell that to the Comanche." He paused, then wondered aloud, "What do you figure he was doing out here all by his lonesome?"

"Maybe he was scouting."

FW Red looked around at me in alarm. "For a raiding party?"

I gave him a wry grin. "Not for no church social."

We reached the Bar F just before sundown and gave out the bad news about Needle and the horses.

Old man French shook his rugged head. "Lordy, Lordy, Lordy. Old Needle. Good man." He looked from FW Red to me. "You didn't catch a look at the bushwhackers, you say?"

"They had us pinned down, Pete," replied FW Red. "Those lead plums was coming at us like a swarm of bees. Then next we knew, they was gone."

Runnels stood behind Pete French, a sneer on his face and a gloating look in his eyes. At that moment, I knew without a doubt that my theory about Runnels were right.

FW Red continued. "We figure they was white. Hobbs found a cigarette paper on the rim."

Runnels snorted. "A cigarette paper? That don't prove nothing." He glared at me defiantly.

I grinned briefly, my eyes fixed on his. Casually, I replied. "I don't know, Runnels. It could prove a lot more than you think."

His forehead knit in a frown. "What do you mean by that?"

"Nothing, except if a jasper asked the right questions about the paper, he might be surprised at his answers."

His frown deepened. "That don't make no sense to me."

I suppressed a grin. Now I had him wondering.

Old man French broke in. "I reckon I'm dumb as a box of hair, Hobbs, but I'm like Runnels. I don't see what good a cigarette paper does for us."

"First, we know they were white. It had rained the night before, which would have caused the paper to fall apart. Whoever dropped it did so after the rain." I glanced at Runnels, who was listening carefully. "Second, when I checked the sign on the rim, I discovered one of the horses had two nails missing from a shoe." I deliberately turned my eyes on Runnels. "Once you find that shoe with the two missing nails, you'll have your bushwhackers."

From the corner of my eye, I saw FW Red glance at me. I ignored him.

Runnels dragged the tip of his tongue over his lips, then shrugged his shoulders and grunted. "And how are you going to do that?"

Innocently, I replied, "Well, I figured by telling you and the boys, we could all keep our eyes peeled.

Never can tell when lowdown, trashy vermin like that might pop up. Isn't that right, Runnels?"

Fire flashed from his eyes. His face grew dark, but he held his temper. Slowly he nodded. "Yeah, I reckon so."

Pete French exclaimed, "Looks like that's about the best we can do." He shook his head. "I sure would like to get my hands on them owlhoots. I don't care about the horses. I'd trade all my horses for Old Needle."

For a moment, I considered telling my idea about why Needle was shot, but I didn't have the proof. It would have to wait until later.

Chapter Eleven

FW Red caught up with me after I left the main
house leading my dun to the barn. "Hey, Hobbs.
Why didn't you tell me about that horseshoe with
the missing nails?"

I grinned down at him. "Because it never happened. I lied. I wanted to give Runnels something
to worry about."

He shoved his hat back and scratched his head.
"Huh?"

We continued toward the barn. "I know you
aren't convinced about Runnels, but I might be able
to prove it if you're willing."

"Shoot."

"If I'm right, as soon as Runnels leaves the old
man, he'll go straight to his boys and tell them

96

about the horseshoe. I'd be willing to bet, they'll hightail to the barn and check their ponies."

His eyes lit with understanding. "And you want me to be there watching, huh?"

"Exactly."

"When?"

I looked around. A couple of the boys, O.C. and Coco, were sauntering toward the chuck house. "Let's put our ponies up. You stay behind in the barn. I'll go on to supper. If anyone asks, I'll tell them you ate something that didn't agree, and you're spending your time between the privy and your bunk."

He grinned and nodded.

"But don't let anyone see you."

Runnels and Barton were in the chuck house when I moseyed in. When I plopped down at the table, other cowhands bombarded me with questions. Three times, I went over what had taken place, and three times I mentioned the missing nails in the horseshoes.

Then Carson showed up. He filled his plate and sat at the end of the table with Runnels and Barton. He leaned forward and whispered to them. Barton looked at Runnels and grinned.

To my surprise, a few minutes later, FW Red ambled in. "Feel better now," he announced. "Figured

I'd see if I could keep some of the beef stew down."
He winked at me as he slid in at the table.

Then the conversation shifted around to the all of
the adventures and misadventures Needle had been
through at the Bar F.

After supper, FW Red and I stood out by the
corral smoking a Bull Durham. "You was right," he
said. "Not ten minutes after I hid up in the loft,
Carson came in. He looked at a chestnut and a pinto.
All four feet." He shook his head. "You plumb sure
hit the nail on the head that time."

"We still need proof," I muttered.

At that moment, the older sister, Alicia, stepped
out on the porch in the glow of the lantern on the
post. I hesitated, staring at her.

FW Red chuckled. "She's a right pretty one."

I grunted. "Reckon so."

He studied my solemn face a moment, then said,
"Won't do you no good. She's got her cap set for
Runnels."

"Runnels?" I looked at him in disbelief.

He shrugged helplessly.

"You serious?"

"As a tick on the back of a hog." He paused and
studied my face in the light of the moon. "Look,
Hobbs. I like you. You appear to be a good man."
He wagged his finger back and forth as if I were a
recalcitrant child. "Gospel truth is that one is spoiled
bad. She carries on like she's better than everyone
else unless she wants something. Then she's all

peaches and cream. Now, if I was the kind looking to settle down, I'd take me a look at Miss Louisa."

"Miss Louisa!" I looked at him in surprise. "She's a little tomboy."

"Maybe so, but more than once, when things got tight or when we got hit by Comanche, she was right there beside us fighting them off while the other one was hiding in her bedroom crying. That little woman has staying power. You best believe it."

I remained silent, not wanting to believe FW Red. Alicia was one of the prettiest women I had ever seen, and in the short time I had been at the Bar F, I had dreamed of what might be with her.

FW Red jerked me from my thoughts. "What are we going to do about Runnels now?"

"We've got to have proof. I can't get it as long as I work here. Runnels watches all of us like a hawk."

He frowned. "What do you mean?"

I flipped my cigarette to the ground and crushed it with the heel of my boot. "I mean, I'm packing my plunder and pulling out."

"You're what?" He looked at me in disbelief.

"That's the only way. Now, remember where we first met up north, back in the hollow among the boulders?"

"Yeah."

"Every three days, about mid-afternoon, I'll be there to fill you in on what I've learned." I gestured

to the west. "Out there somewhere, Runnels is holding stolen stock. Once I find it, I'll take the old man
out to see for himself."

FW Red studied a moment on my idea, then nodded and offered his hand. "You be careful, Hobbs.
Mighty careful."

"I'll be careful. You keep your mouth closed. No
one needs to know what we're up to."

Pete French leaned back in his cushioned wing-
back chair and absently tapped his pipe in the palm
of his hand after I told him I was quitting. Mrs.
French stared at me in surprise. He growled, "Hate
to lose you, Hobbs. You're a good hand."

"Thanks, Mister French. I reckon I just got itchy
feet. I didn't want to ride out without thanking you
and your family," I said, looking around at Little
Pete and his sisters who stood in the open doorway
between the kitchen and parlor. The boy looked like
he wanted to cry. Miss Louisa chewed on her bottom lip, but to my disappointment, Alicia gave
every sign of being bored.

"You can't go, Lew," Little Pete begged. "You
got all kinds of stuff to teach me."

I shook my head, hating the anguish I was caus-
ing the boy even though my intentions were to help
the entire family. "Sorry, Sprout. There's country
out there to see, and I want to see my share of it."

The old man wanted to pay me for what little

time I had worked, but I refused, asking instead for a couple days of grub.

He rose stiffly from his chair and offered his hand. "Tell Cookie to give you the grub. And if you're ever looking for a spot, they'll always be one here for you."

Miss Louisa spoke up. "Take care of yourself, Lew." Her bottom lip quivered.

I nodded to her and looked at Alicia. She gave me a faint smile and turned back into the kitchen.

When I made my announcement in the bunkhouse, Runnels quickly covered his surprise with a smug grin. He was figuring he'd seen the last of me, but he was in for a surprise.

I rode out north with a warm spot inside of me for the Frenches, although I was puzzled over the way Alicia had acted. I reckoned she was still feeling sick from last Sunday.

After picking my way along the shore of the Frio for a couple miles, I made a cold camp back in the boulders. I rose before sunrise, boiled some coffee, gnawed on a cold biscuit, and rode out, planning on making another six or eight miles before climbing from the canyon and heading back south.

At mid-afternoon, I topped out on the rim. My first task was to return to the dead lawman back south and bury him. By the time I reached him, there was nothing but bones remaining. I buried them beneath the sand. I stood looking down at the small grave. "Sorry, Pardner. I wish I could have done more."

Swinging back into the saddle, I moved out. Rolling hills covered with cedar and rock spread as far as the eye could see. I rode at the base of the hills, not wanting to skyline myself. At the same time, some of the countryside was so rugged, an hombre would have to ride right up on another before seeing him.

A few miles on, the lay of the land smoothed some, offering more of a view, and that was when I spotted the small herd of cows moving west.

I eased up the back of a hill and made my way to the top, reining up behind a cedar. The herd was about a mile away, too far to make out the identity of the cowpoke pushing the animals. There appeared to be five or six head in the bunch.

The remainder of the day I tagged along, keeping an eye on the small herd. I camped that night when they camped, and moved out the next morning with the herd. Around noon, I paused on the side of a hill, making sure the crest was between me and the cowpoke moving the herd.

To the west, I spotted another canyon, this one over a mile wide. "So this is where they keep them," I said to my pony. "Their own little canyon." I moved around to keep an eye on the herd as it paused at the rim, then disappeared down a trail.

After the rider disappeared, I cautiously approached the rim, dismounting several yards before reaching it. Lying on my belly, I peered over the side. There was another river running through the canyon, which appeared very similar to Frio Canyon.

Through the green canopy of treetops a few hundred feet below, the rider pushed the small herd up the canyon. The tangle of branches made identifying him impossible. His voice, too faint and broken to recognize, drifted up as he urged the cows steadily northward.

"A box canyon somewhere," I muttered to myself, surmising that was his destination with the animal: a box canyon where a few rails across the mouth would be all that was necessary to contain a herd of stolen beef.

Part of me wanted to follow as soon as he was out of sight, but the other side cautioned patience. Chances were he would soon return. If he didn't then I could follow. Five or six head of beeves leave enough sign so I couldn't lose their trail.

An hour later, I heard the echo of steel shoes clicking on rocks below. I squinted through the canopy of leaves and branches. Moments later, the rider reappeared.

Quickly, I backed away, climbed into the saddle, and headed for the nearest cedar-covered hill some half-mile distant from the trail he rode in on. I wanted to get a better look at him.

From a hidden vantage point near the crest, I dismounted and waited. Once my rustler had disappeared back to the east, I'd ride down and see what I could find.

The wind was from the south, so I pinched my horse's nostrils. Last thing I needed was for Old Bill to nicker when he caught the smell of another horse.

"There he is," I whispered to Bill. "But who?"

I squinted my eyes. He had the same build as both Carson and Barton. It could have been either. Then I made out the Montana crown on his hat. Carson! My pulse raced, pumping adrenaline through my veins. I was right. All my guesses had been right. Carson rode a chestnut, and though the distance was too great to discern exactly the color of the horse before me, it could very well be chestnut.

I waited until long after Carson had disappeared before I headed for the trail. I shucked my Winchester as I started down. The trail was much narrower that the one leading out of Frio Canyon, but this one gave plenty evidence that it was heavily used.

At the base of the trail, I eased into a tangle of cedar so I could study the lay of the land without fear of being spotted. To my surprise, I found a cave that gave evidence of having been used more than once.

Satisfied no one was watching, I headed north, staying under the trees and avoiding rocky areas when I could.

Since Barton had taken an hour to drop the cattle

off and then return, I guessed the box canyon to be a mile, maybe a tad more, from the trail. I moved cautiously. After about half a mile or so, I picked up the pungent odor of woodsmoke. I dismounted and tied Bill in a patch of scrub oak and willow thickets. Then, leaning the Winchester against a tree, I unfolded my gunbelt from the saddlebags.

For all things there came a time and place, I told myself, staring at the worn leather holster and belt. This was that time and that place. I strapped on the gunbelt and slid the .44 Colt from the holster. I checked the chamber, spun it once or twice, listening with satisfaction at the reassuring smooth clicks as the cylinder spun.

I looked up at Bill, who was watching me with his large brown eyes. "Been a spell since I had this on, huh, Boy?"

Holstering the Colt and retrieving my Winchester, I moved out, darting from tree to tree, trying to keep a dark background behind me.

Fifteen minutes later, I spotted the source of the smoke: a small, shabby cabin built against the rocky bluff next to the mouth of the box canyon.

Carefully, I eased closer. The mouth of the box canyon was less than twenty feet wide, sealed off by a wood rail fence laid out in a zigzag pattern, what I heard called a Virginia rail fence during the war as we fought through Virginia. Chances were, it opened into a large valley, completely enclosed by sheer walls of limestone.

There were no windows in the cabin, only the door for me to worry about. Gradually I drew closer to the fence. Next to the fence where it joined the rock wall of the cliff grew a large oak, old and ancient, its trunk at least five feet in diameter. I studied the cabin, then the distance I had to cover to the oak. Fifteen feet or so. Three seconds, maybe four.

Taking a deep breath, I dashed across the small clearing for the oak. I pressed my back up against rough bark when I reached the tree, gasping for breath. Moving only my head, I turned and peered into the box canyon. I had been right once again. It opened into a valley almost a mile long and just as wide, and dotting the graze inside were at least a hundred head of stock.

Suddenly the door of the cabin scraped open. I froze, my ears straining to pick up the sound of footsteps. A series of hacking coughs carried across the clearing. I peered around the side of the oak.

My eyes bulged. Ike Bailey! So this was where he had disappeared.

Despite my uncomfortable predicament, I couldn't help grinning. All I had to do now was get back to Pete French and show him what I had discovered.

As I spied on Ike, he went back inside. As soon as the door slammed shut behind him, I broke into a run for my horse.

*   *   *

I awakened Pete French early in the morning. With a lantern in his hand, he opened the door. Before he could say a word, I said, "You've got to listen to me, Pete. I found the men who've been stealing your cattle, and I know where they're hiding them."

He looked at me like I was crazy. "Hobbs. You know what time it is?"

"This is important, Pete."

He shook his head wearily. "Well, come on in." He led the way into the parlor and turned to face me. He set the lantern on an end table by the round-backed couch. "Now, what's all this about rustling? I ain't been rustled. Not lately. Comanche might steal one or two, but that's it."

I shook my head. "You've been rustled, Pete, and you don't know it. I can show you over a hundred head of your stock waiting to be driven up to the Goodnight-Loving or Chisholm Trail and sold to drives pushing north to the Navaho reservation at Fort Sumner or on to Kansas."

"Where?"

I pointed west. "I don't know the name, but there's a canyon several hours ride to the west."

He nodded. "Nueces Canyons."

"That's where they are. In a box canyon, and Ike Bailey is the one looking after them."

"Bailey!"

"And I saw Carson riding away from there earlier

today. He probably got in here only a couple hours back."

That got his attention. "I heard some commotion out in the barn. Thought the dogs might be chasing a coon or possum."

"It was Carson."

He studied me several seconds, skeptical of my claims. "Just who's behind this so-called rustling?"

I knew he wouldn't believe me, but I had to tell him, and then hope he would still accompany me to the box canyon.

"Bart Runnels."

Before Pete French could reply, a rifle boomed. Pete jerked back, a sudden blossom of blood appearing on his nightshirt. His eyes grew wide, and he stared at me in disbelief. His gaze traveled down to my six-gun still in the holster. He staggered back, looking into my eyes, his own filled with confusion. He tried to form the word *who,* but he stumbled backward over the couch and sprawled to the floor.

Chapter Twelve

My ears rang from the gunshot as I shucked my six-gun and spun around. I fired at the window from where the shot came. I heard a yell. In the next moment, Mrs. French rushed in. When she saw her husband sprawled on the floor, she fell to her knees by his side, screaming.

I hurried to help, but when she looked up at me, she recoiled and hissed, "Murderer! Killer!"

I stared at her dumbly. "No. No. Not me." When I looked up, Alicia Miss Louisa, and Little Pete were staring at me in horror. I shook my head. "I didn't do it. I—"

Shouts from outside interrupted me. I glanced around and realized no one would believe me. I had to escape and somehow try to find the real killer. I looked back at Little Pete. I shook my head. "I

didn't do it, Little Pete. You got to believe me."
And then I sprinted for the door.

I fired a couple shots over the heads of the dark
figures racing toward the main house and leaped
into my saddle. I headed north. The only thought
that made any sense of the confusion bouncing
around in my head was that I had to put as much
distance between me and the ranch as I could.

I was still moving at sunup. Bill was beginning
to tire. I'd worked him mighty hard the last couple
days. Then I recognized the spot where FW Red
and I had camped, the spot we had planned to meet
at. Would he still come?

Reining up at the water's edge, I let Bill drink, but
not much. A foundered horse would mean a surefire
necktie party for me. I pulled his head up. "Take it
easy, Fella. You can have some more later."

I crossed the river and found a spot where I could
watch for FW Red, a spot that had a narrow trail
leading to the top of the rim. Though I loosened
Bill's cinch, I left the saddle on him.

Suddenly, I was hungry. Last I'd eaten was
breakfast the day before. My stomach was so empty
it rattled against my backbone. I had some grub left
from what Cookie had packed me.

Two hours later, FW Red showed up. I watched
his back trail as he wandered aimlessly around
where we had camped. When I was satisfied he was
alone, I gave a whistle.

FW Red reined up and stared across the river. I whistled again, and he urged his pony forward. I stepped from behind a tree and gestured for him to come over.

I led the way through a thicket of cedar to a clearing in a cluster of boulders.

"I figured you'd be up here," he said, dismounting.

"I hoped as much." His eyes settled on my sidearm. He looked up at me. "Sometimes there's no choice," I said.

He nodded slowly. "Who shot old Pete?"

"I don't know. I found the rustled cattle. I told Pete about them. I wanted him to see for himself when somebody shot him through the window."

"You think they were shooting at him or you?"

"I wasn't more than ten feet from the window. I don't see how they could have missed me, just like I didn't miss the shooter."

FW Red's eyes widened. "What's that?"

"I got off a shot. I hit whoever was out there. I heard him yell."

His eyes narrowed. "Why that dirty—"

"Who?"

"Carson. He had a bullet graze on his right shoulder. He said he got it when you shot at them when they was running to the main house."

I shook my head. "I shot over their heads. Deliberately. The only way he could have got that wound is when I shot the bushwhacker at the window."

FW Red cursed. "Now all we got to do is prove it."

"What we have to do first is save the herd."

He frowned. "What do you mean?"

"Carson had to overhear what I told Pete. How much would you be willing to bet that Runnels has already sent him and Barton to help Bailey move the stolen cows?"

"Bailey? Is he in on this?"

"He's in the Nueces Canyons. The cows are in a box canyon. Like I told Pete. I figure they rustled them in small bunches over a few months, then come early spring, they'd sell the beef to cattle drives pushing up to the Indian reservations in New Mexico or maybe on to Denver."

Suddenly Bill's ears perked forward, and FW Red's horse turned his head. Across the river came the whinny of a horse. I held my finger to my lips. "Stay here. You don't need to be seen. You're my only hope of getting out of this mess." I eased forward and peered through the underbrush.

I groaned. It was Little Pete, all by his lonesome.

For a moment, I considered letting him ride past, but I didn't want him to think I was the one who killed his pa. I whistled, then stepped out.

With a grin, he spurred his pony across the river. "Lew. I was hoping I'd find you." His eyes danced with excitement.

"How'd you get up here?"

"I followed FW Red." He looked around. "Is he here?"

"This way," I replied, taking the bridle and leading his pony through the cedar.

"Little Pete!" FW Red exclaimed.

The young boy beamed. "Hi, FW Red. I been following you. I hoped you'd find Lew."

"You all by yourself?" I glanced in the direction of his back trail.

"Yeah. Coco and O.C. are somewhere behind me. I don't know how far."

I grimaced. "That means we don't have much time. Now, listen, Little Pete. I want to tell you what happened."

He shook his head. "I know you didn't kill Pa, Lew. You ain't that kind of man."

"Thanks, but you need to know what took place." Quickly, I went back over the story, the rustlers, Bailey, and finally the fateful meeting with his pa. "I didn't like telling you all that, Boy, but you've got to be a man. You'll have you a ranch to run."

He grimaced.

"What is it?"

Little Pete gulped. "It ain't good, Lew. Just this morning, I overheard Runnels talking to Alicia about how once they were married, he would be running the ranch."

My eyes bulged in disbelief. "What?"

FW Red clucked his tongue. Reluctantly, he reminded me. "I told you she had her cap set for Runnels. Remember?"

Trying to conceal my pain, I shrugged. "Yeah, I remember. It just caught me by surprise."

"One thing for certain, Runnels ain't wasting no time."

He was right about that. I looked up at Little Pete. "You ride back and keep an eye on things at the ranch. FW Red and me will try to bring the cattle back."

FW Red frowned at me. "And how do you reckon we'll do that?"

I took a deep breath. "I don't know. We'll just have to figure something out. All I know is we've got to try."

He gave me a crooked grin. "I reckon you know we're playing with a short deck."

"You mind?"

His grin grew wider. "Not particularly."

I tightened the cinch and swung into the saddle. "Let's go then."

During the day, gray clouds moved in. Throughout the afternoon they grew darker, a portent of bad weather. Soon the ominous rumble of thunder rolled across the prairie. Just before sunset, the first of the rain struck.

"There!" FW Red exclaimed, pointing to the west. "There's the canyon."

"Let's get to the bottom while we can see," I said,

pulling my Stetson down tighter on my head and urging Bill into a lope. "Once the light's gone, it'll be darker than the inside of a cow."

The rain intensified. By the time we reached the trail down the side of the canyon, we could only see a few feet ahead of us. I dismounted. "Let's lead them down. I'll go first. There's a cave at the bottom of the trail. It'll do for tonight."

By the time we reached the bottom of the trail, the night had grown so dark that I had to hold my hand in front of me as I pushed through the cedar toward the wall of the bluff. FW Red was right behind, leading his pony and holding on to Bill's tail so as not to get lost.

"Hold up!" I yelled through the rain when I felt the canyon wall. Slowly, I felt along the wall, searching for the mouth of the cave.

"You sure you know where that cave is?" FW Red called out.

"Unless some jasper has come along and plugged it up," I shouted. And then my hand touched space. I halted abruptly and felt around. Pulling my hand back, I touched the limestone bluff. I felt forward again, exploring. It was the cave mouth. "Here it is," I said, leading the way just inside out of the rain.

As soon as we were out of the rain, I cautioned FW Red. "Don't go stomping into the dark until we see what we got in here. I reckon a nice cool cave like this could be home to a few snakes." I fumbled in my saddlebags to tear off a piece of paper in which Cookie had wrapped my grub. I touched a match to it, and a welcome flame illumined the mouth of the cave.

I spotted no snakes, but I grinned like the proverbial possum when I did spot dry, broken limbs lying about. Within minutes, we had us a small fire, providing warmth from the chill of the rain and comfort for two cowpokes hoping to carry out a long and dangerous task.

The rain grew harder.

A cigarette dangling from his lips, FW Red lay on his saddle blanket, which he had tossed over his saddle. He cut his eyes toward the mouth of the cave. "How far do you reckon we're above the river?"

I listened to the rushing waters, audible beneath the pounding of the rain. "Not far. Three, maybe four feet."

"You thinking what I'm thinking?"

"About the rain? Yep."

Staring at the rain, he muttered, "More than once, I saw the Frio stretching out to half a mile," he said, his voice soft and wondering. "Mighty wide."

"Well, look at it this way. It might be wide, but it's shallow. Even if the river spread from canyon to canyon, it shouldn't be more than a foot or so over here. Come morning, if we see we got a problem, we'll take the trail back up and follow along the rim."

I always slept soundly to the steady beat of rain, but that night I awakened several times, and each time the pounding rush of river grew louder and louder.

Morning crept in, managing to ease the darkness of the storm. The rain continued. I stood in the mouth of the cave, studying the water swirling past the base of the cedars a few feet away. Behind me, I heard FW Red stirring. "Looks like you were right. Water's rising."

He muttered a curse. "Just our blasted luck."

I flipped my cigarette out into the rain and turned back to my horse. "I reckon we best get while the getting's good. Looks like now, our best bet is to follow on the rim."

Saddling quickly, we were ready to ride when from upriver came a distant roar punctuated by sharp cracks like gunshots. FW Red looked at me in alarm.

"Let's get," I said, swinging into the saddle and spurring Bill through the cedar to the trail. FW Red stayed closer to me than two coats of paint.

We had climbed no more than ten feet up the trail when a wall of water, sounding like a locomotive, came crashing past. We moved a little higher before pausing.

FW Red shook his head. Despite the rain cascading down, his face was pale. "We just did make it," he muttered in relief. Suddenly, he stood in his stirrups. "Hey, what's that out there? Looks like part of a house or something."

"Looks like part of the cabin Ike Bailey was living in."

Chapter Thirteen

The rain continued to fall as we stood on the trail, watching the swift brown waters rush past. "What about the cows?" FW Red pointed to the shattered fragments of the cabin being swept away. "I don't see any out there."

I grimaced. If the flood had caught Bailey by surprise, he would not have even considered taking time to turn the stolen cows loose. That could mean they were still trapped in the box canyon, fated to drown if the water rose too high. "We'd best take a look." I leaned forward and touched my heels to Bill's flank.

He lumbered up the steep slope.

On the rim, we cut north. "Sure could use a cigarette," FW Red muttered, pulling his head deeper into the upturned collar of his slicker.

I pointed north. "Straight ahead, we'll run across the box canyon. We can look down and see if the cows are there."

"What if they ain't?"

I glanced at smaller man. "That means Runnels sent Barton and Carson out not long after Old Pete was killed with orders to move the herd, fast."

Twenty minutes later, we reined up on the rim of the box canyon. Floodwaters covered the canyon, but not so deep as to prevent our seeing that a section of the rail fence had been removed. "They must've got the herd out of the canyon just before the rain hit," I said.

"But we didn't see them."

"They took them north. We'll follow the rim. If we don't find sign on this side, then we'll swing around and track the west side of the canyon."

Around noon, the rain slacked off. By evening, the clouds had moved out. FW Red muttered a curse. "I never thought I'd say it, but I've had all the rain I can take. I'm afraid to take off my boots for fear my toes have growed webs like a duck."

I laughed. "Well, look at the bright side. With web feet you could lead an easy life in a circus showing your toes off."

He growled, "Not me. Ain't no way I'd be one of them sideshow people."

As we continued north toward the headsprings of the Nueces, the canyon became shallower. Making a cold camp that night, we pushed out early next morning and continued north, seeing no sign of the herd. By late afternoon, we came to the headsprings of the Nueces on the border of Edwards and Real counties where the Frio Canyon was nothing but a jumble of rocks.

FW Red scratched his three-day beard. "Looks like they came out on the west side of the canyon."

Dismounting for a drink of cold water and to re-fill my canteen, I agreed. "Likely they're heading north to the Goodnight-Loving Trail. If we cut due west, we should cut their sign."

FW Red lay on his belly sipping the cold water. He splashed it on his face and looked up at me. "Unless we're ahead of them, which means we could miss them."

I arched an eyebrow. "You're just full of good thoughts, aren't you?"

He grinned. "Trying to help, that's all. Just trying to help."

"Well, you're right." I chuckled. "I'd be right upset if we missed them just because we pulled ahead of the herd. Maybe we should head southwest."

That night, as I lay staring at the stars, I was filled with the disturbing thought that we might never find the herd nor the rustlers.

I knew that was a foolish idea, for a hundred or so head of beef leave plenty of signs. But still, I worried. I tried to push my fears aside, and when I did, Alicia and Runnels popped into my mind. A sharp pain of anguish stabbed me in the chest. Despite FW Red's warning about her, I couldn't shake Alicia French from my thoughts.

We moved out with the false dawn, heading southwest. As the sun peeked over the horizon, we pulled up just below the crest of a hill and studied the rolling landscape covered with cedar and mesquite.

"One thing for certain," FW Red muttered. "We best not count on spotting them. Why you could hide a thousand head of cows out there and not lay an eye on them for a month."

He was right. "Tell you what. Let's move back to the rim and head due south. Sooner or later, we've got to run across the sign where they came out of the canyon. Then we can follow the trail."

We hit the canyon at noon. FW Red glanced over the rim. "Canyon sure is shallow here. What do you figure, forty or fifty feet?"

"Probably. Nowhere close to the two or three hundred back at the cave."

I blamed myself for what happened next. I was too busy studying the canyon than paying attention to what was going on around me.

Without warning, booming gunshots broke the silence. The next few seconds seemed like years. Squealing in terror, Bill reared, pawing at the sky with his front feet. A powerful blow struck my shoulder, sending me tumbling from my saddle. At the same time, Bill spun around, and when his front feet came down, the edge of the rim crumbled, sending him plunging over the precipice.

I tried to shout, but I was falling. I heard Bill squealing, and the last thing I remember was trying to grab at anything to break my fall. And then all went black.

It was dark when I awakened. I lay motionless, trying to gather my thoughts. I wasn't sure if I were dead or alive, for I could see nothing. For a moment, I couldn't remember just what had taken place. Then slowly, the pieces began to fit themselves together in my pounding skull.

I blinked to focus my eyes. Directly overhead was pitch black, but by shifting my gaze to the right, I glimpsed stars. I had fallen into a crevice and rolled under a ledge of some sort. When I struggled to move, a searing pain ripped through my shoulder. I caught my breath and groaned.

Next I knew, the sun had risen. I moved only my eyes, hoping to avoid some of the pain I'd experienced earlier. My head throbbed. I mumbled, "You must be alive, Lew. Nobody who is dead could hurt this much."

From where I lay, I could see the rim of the crevice about fifteen feet above my head. When I hit bottom, I must have rolled under the ledge. I figured if there were anything positive from being bushwhacked, it was that I rolled under the ledge, which might have prevented the bushwhackers from giving me a finishing shot.

FW Red! What had happened to him? And then I remembered seeing Bill plunge over the rim. I grimaced. "Well, you got yourself in one predicament this time, Lew Hobbs. So maybe you best set yourself about getting out of it."

Clenching my teeth against the pain, I shifted my shoulders to the right and froze as searing pain exploded in my shoulder. I held myself rigid, waiting for the pain to subside. Sweat popped out on my forehead, and I gasped for breath. "Breathe deep. Breathe deep," I muttered.

After a few moments, I moved my hips and legs. The pain struck again, but not with the intensity of the first time.

I shifted my torso again, and again went rigid with the pain. I'd only moved a few inches, but I told myself if I could move an inch, I could move a foot, or two feet.

And slowly, muttering oaths at the pain and those who had caused it, I managed to slide from under the ledge. Now all I had to do was sit up, then stand, and then—I was too exhausted to plan any further. I blinked my eyes against the bright sun.

With a Herculean effort, I managed to sit upright. Leaning back against the side of the crevice, I closed my eyes and gasped for breath. My left shoulder throbbed, radiating pain to every part of my body. Blood caked my shirt.

Opening my eyes, I studied the crevice into which I had fallen. For an hombre with two good arms, climbing out was no trouble, but with only one, I was going to have a problem.

Slowly, the pain eased. Eyes closed, I remained motionless for several minutes, enjoying the respite from the slashing pain. At the same time, I knew I had to climb from the crevice and tend to the wound in my shoulder. Infection is an insidious offspring of gun wounds, often killing as many as the slugs themselves.

So, clenching my teeth, I struggled to my feet, cursing the pain. At the narrow end of the crevice, I leaned my shoulders against one wall and placed my feet on the other. I'd take a step or two, then scoot my back up a few inches. Slowly, I worked my way up the wall, step by step.

By the time I reached the top, my shoulder felt like someone was running a red-hot poker back and forth through it. All I could do was lie on the ground and pray for the pain to go away, at the same time knowing it would continue growing worse until I tended the wound.

I managed to stagger to the rim, taking care not to stand too close lest I pass out and topple over the edge. I peered below and grimaced when I spotted Bill through the canopy of branches and leaves. Tears filled my eyes. He had been a good friend and a dependable mount.

A dark object appeared through the leaves, and

then another, and then a third. I squinted, hoping to get a better look. I shouted a curse when I realized they were buzzards going about their grisly task on Bill. With my good arm, I hurled rocks at them, driving them into the air.

At the same time, another five or six buzzards lumbered into the air less than fifty feet north of Bill. A cold chill ran up my spine as I stumbled along the rim for a better look, yet fearful of what I would find.

A horse. FW Red's horse.

I closed my eyes and dropped my chin to my chest in despair. I don't know whether FW Red was shot or whether he died in the fall, but now I had two reasons to somehow find a way down into the canyon. First was to bury FW Red and second, to take care of my shoulder.

Stumbling along the rim, I paused every few steps to catch my breath. I spent an hour covering a hundred yards before I found a narrow fissure that appeared to slope to the canyon floor. Given my weakened condition, the fissure was too steep for me to risk descending on my feet, so I sat on my rump and scooted down, wincing and muttering as shards of limestone and granite jabbed me.

The fissure ended ten feet off the canyon floor, which meant I had to jump. I studied the ten feet, telling myself ruefully that to make the day perfect for me, all I had to do now was break a leg.

I lay back on the slope and dangled my legs over

the edge. Slowly, using my hips and back, I scooted down so that when gravity pulled me I'd only have about five or six feet to fall.

I landed in a soft bed of gravel and leaves. My arm continued to throb, but I had grown accustomed to the pain and could now force myself to think despite it. I headed back toward the horses.

Frowning at the job the buzzards had done on FW Red's pony, I started searching for him. He was nowhere to be found. I looked around, even searching the trees in case his body had lodged in a fork. I found nothing. Could he have somehow lived through the fall?

A fresh spasm of pain reminded me to do what I could for my arm.

I tried not to look at Bill as I removed my saddlebags and Winchester. I studied the saddle. I couldn't slide it off the dead horse, not with one arm. Still, I loosened the cinch. It wasn't much to do for Bill, but I figured that would make him a little more comfortable.

Heading south, I discovered a secluded spot under a rocky ledge. I built a fire and boiled water. I washed the wound as clean as I could. The flesh around it was red, an indication of early infection. Without medicine, all I could do was keep the wound clean.

I couldn't stay here.

And I was in no condition to travel.

Chapter Fourteen

W hile I wasn't hungry, I knew I had to eat. All I had was a few strips of jerky. More than once, I'd managed on jerky and water. *No reason not to this time,* I told myself as I put more water on to boil and cut up a couple slices of jerky for the pot. Nothing fancy, but jerky broth would keep the hunger away and the strength up.

I spent a restless night. My shoulder burned, and my face was hot to the touch. Twice during the night, I washed the bullet hole in my shoulder.

When the sun rose, I was exhausted from lack of sleep and pain. My shoulder had grown so tender, so sore, that the slightest touch was excruciating. I knew what that meant. I had seen it with others. And now, it was me.

I managed to sit up against the rough bark of a

live oak. Overhead, a few white clouds drifted along in the blue sky. Strange how a jasper admires objects when he realizes he might never see them again. I was tired, so tired. I closed my eyes, planning on a few minutes' rest before beginning my journey down river—to where, I had no idea. All I knew was that if I remained where I was, I would die.

I awakened with a start when hands gently shook me. "Hobbs. Hobbs. Wake up. It's me. FW Red."

My eyes refused to focus. I shook my head. "FW Red? Is that you?" My voice was weak and hoarse.

"Yeah, Pardner. It's me. And I got us some help."

I stared up at him in disbelief. "It is you." A grin leaped to my face. "I'll bet—it really is you."

He laughed. "Yeah, and look who else is here." He moved aside for me to see Run With Horse staring at me impassively, his left arm bandaged.

With him were several warriors with long hair, all staring at me with black eyes. Run With Horse barked some orders and the warriors busied themselves building up the fire and pulled a hindquarter of venison from one of the horses. He himself knelt and inspected my wound. His face darkened. He touched it with the back of his fingers. "Not good," he said.

He fished around in his parfleche bag and pulled out a small clove. "Eat. Peyote."

I gladly ate. When I could get my hands on peyote, I carried it with me. It deadened pain so a body could rest and rebuild his strength.

A second warrior handed him a cup, which he passed to me. "Drink. Will help wound." Within minutes I began to relax, and then Run With Horse motioned yet another warrior forward, an older Comanche. He inspected my wound, grunted, then opened a leather bag and pulled out two or three different roots. He ground them between two rocks until they were pulverized, then made a thick white paste with water.

"Take out poison," Run With Horse explained, nodding to the paste. "Good."

I jerked back when the older warrior coated my shoulder with the mixture. It had a burning, astringent effect. I could almost feel the poison being sucked from the wound.

FW Red spoke up. "You and me are two lucky hombres, Hobbs. By all rights, we should be dead."

Sweat began to pour from my skin. The effects of the medicine, I guessed. I licked my lips. "I reckon you're right."

"I sure thought I was a goner when my horse went over the rim. Would have been too except I bounced off a couple high limbs in one of them old oaks and got myself lodged in a fork about halfway down. I looked around for you, but all I found was your horse. I waited around until night and then decided to head for the Bar F." He nodded to Run With Horse. "Run into our friend here the next day.

They fed me, doctored up my cuts and scratches, and then we come looking for you."

I forced a grin. "I'm mighty glad you did."

He grew somber. "You figure it was Carson and Barton that shot at us?"

"Who else?

"That's what I figured. So what do we do now?"

The older warrior sat back on his haunches and nodded to Run With Horse. He then took a length of grass rope and looped it around my neck as a sling for my arm. "Not move arm," he muttered.

I nodded. "Thanks."

"Like I said," FW Red repeated. "What next?"

"The herd. We've still got to get the herd."

A frown wrinkled his forehead. He rubbed his fingers over his several-day-old beard. "You ain't in no shape to ride."

I looked at Run With Horse. "Men who did this stole a herd of cows. Help me get cows back, and I give you ten head." I held up my hand, fingers spread, twice.

The warriors moved off to the side and for several minutes were involved in a heated discussion. Finally, Run With Horse turned back to me. "We help."

I grinned at FW Red and nodded to Run With Horse. "Thanks. I figure they're heading north."

Solemnly, he acknowledged the information. "We find." He spoke to a young warrior who listened silently, then nodded. "This Big Knee. He will remain with you until the next sun. Then he will lead you to us."

"To you? But where are you going?"

He gestured to the north. "We ride tonight. We find herd." He jabbed his finger at me and FW Red. "You follow tomorrow."

Before I could question him further, FW Red spoke up. "We got a couple extra ponies. Mustangs, but they're tough little boogers. We can pull the gear off our horses in the morning."

I relaxed. Whether it was the medicine, the peyote, or the fact we were once again after the herd, I don't know. Maybe a combination of all three. Whatever it was, I relaxed, and when I did, my stomach growled. "I don't know about you, but I'm hungry."

Broiled venison has almost no fat so it isn't a filling as fattier meats, but that night it tasted like a T-bone steak with all the trimmings. As I leaned back and patted my stomach, I noticed FW Red wore a black eye. "How come you got a shiner on that eye?"

He tore a chunk of venison off and chuckled. "When I hit the tree on the way down is all I can figure. I must have bounced my noggin off a limb. I lost my hat, but I was plumb lucky. Other than the eye and the hat, I only had a few cuts and bruises. What about you? What happened to you?"

I filled him in on my tumbling into the crevice and how I managed to climb out.

Before Run With Horse rode out with the others, he left me a handful of peyote cloves. "For shoulder," he explained.

Before turning in that night, I chewed another clove. I slept better than I had in years.

I tied a neckerchief about my head before we rode out early next morning. I had filled my belly with venison, so I was feeling right pert. Big Knee led us to the northwest as if he knew the exact location of his destination.

Two or three times during the day, we paused for a break. The redness had disappeared from around my wound. I didn't know what roots the older warrior had used for the healing paste, but I figured if I could get my hands on them, I'd be rich.

Mid-afternoon, Big Knee reined up on the crest of a hill. He pointed northwest. There, a mile or so distant, a cloud of dust sat on the ground, and in the middle was the herd of cattle plodding toward us. FW Red shouted, "Look at that! Would you just look at that?"

We rode to meet the herd.

Run With Horse rode point. He nodded when we reined up. "Here cows."

I held the reins in my left hand and offered him my right. "Thanks."

He frowned a moment, then realized I wanted to shake his hand. For the first time since we had met him, he grinned and shook my hand. "We find only one man. We kill him."

FW Red and I exchanged puzzled looks. "One? What did he look like?"

The Comanche warrior shrugged. "Hard to say. Look like all white men."

Using my hand, I pantomimed a large stomach. "Fat? Big?"

He studied me a moment, then shook his head. Holding his hands a couple inches apart, he made an up-and-down motion. "Like a snake."

"Bailey!" I exclaimed, looking at FW Red. "That has to be Bailey, which means Carson and Barton got away."

"And probably hightailing it back to the Bar F as fast as they can."

The Comanche warriors had treated us with respect out of deference to the aid we had provided one of their own. But they moved at their own pace, refusing to hurry. Just before sunset, Run With Horse pointed the herd toward a cluster of trees a mile or so distant. "Water," he said. "We camp there tonight."

I started to protest, to insist we make as many miles as we could, but I realized that we were still a few days from the Bar F. No sense in killing the cattle or our horses. Runnels would be waiting for us whenever we arrived.

* * *

During the night, we awakened when another band of Comanche warriors rode in. When they spotted FW Red and me, their faces grew dark and angry. One or two war yelps sounded from the rear of the party, but they were stayed when Run With Horse held up both arms for silence, then spoke rapidly in a dialect I had never encountered.

The anger faded from their faces, but not the inherent mistrust of the white man. Run With Horse gestured to the fire and the hindquarter of beef from which strips of meat had been sliced and broiled over the fire.

FW Red leaned his shoulder into mine and whispered, "Best sleep with your hogleg in your hand the rest of the night, Hobbs."

I whispered back. "Wouldn't help. You'd be lucky to get one shot off." With that, I lay my head back on my saddle and pulled the blanket up about my neck.

When we awakened before sunrise, the newcomers had already ridden out. Run With Horse explained. "They Comanche *Yap Eaters*." He gestured north. "They go other side Red River." As he spoke, two of his warriors cut out the ten head of cattle I'd promised. "They take to our *rancheria* while we take others to yours."

FW Red and I rode at point with Run With Horse. I gestured to the north. "Those *Yap Eaters,* you say they live up north?"

He grunted. "Beyond territory your government made for Indian." He rode in silence a few minutes, then gave us a brief history of the Comanche tribe.

The southernmost band was the *Penateka* or the *Honey Eaters.* North of them were the *Nokonis,* or *Those Who Turn Back.* Sharing the same range as the *Nokonis* were the *Tanima,* the *Liver Eaters,* and the *Tenawas,* also known as *Those Who Stay Downstream.*

Farther north were the *Kotsotekas,* the *Buffalo Eaters,* and beyond them was the range of the band that had passed through during the night, the *Yamparikas.*

FW Red interrupted. "I reckon I understand the meaning of *Liver Eaters* and *Buffalo Eaters,* but what the Sam Hill is a *Yap Eater*?"

His eyes constantly scanning the horizon, Run With Horse replied, "Roots."

"Roots?" FW Red frowned.

The Comanche leader nodded. "Dig from ground. Eat much of."

The redheaded cowpoke grimaced. "Don't sound none too appetizing."

In the beginning the Comanche warriors had remained distant and aloof, carrying out Run With Horse's orders efficiently and ignoring us completely. On the second night, two drank from our canteen, and one accepted a portion of FW Red's broiled steak. On the third, one pointed out the color of FW Red's hair to the others. We couldn't understand their jabbering, but from the grins on their faces, we figured they must be having themselves a good time at Red's expense.

Even Run With Horse wore an amused smile at their gaiety.

As I watched the Comanches carry on over FW Red's curly hair, my hand slid down to the butt of my Colt. I felt a surge of reassurance in my determination not to wear a gun unless the situation was absolutely necessary.

I lifted my gaze and stared into the night, thinking now of Bart Runnels and how he and his kind had plundered and killed a fine old man. I knew I had to keep the gunbelt strapped around my waist. At least until Runnels got what was coming to him.

Next day, FW Red scanned the country around us. "Looks familiar. We ought to reach the trail down the canyon by dark."

"Maybe we best hold them on the rim tonight until we can get a handle on what's taking place back at the ranch."

He nodded and chewed on his bottom lip thoughtfully. "I don't reckon Runnels will be any too pleased to see us."

"I don't reckon he will."

"What kind of play do you reckon he'll make when he sees we ain't dead?"

He had me there. All I could do was shake my head and mutter, "Hard to say. He could deny everything. I don't think that would wash with Mrs. French or Louisa. I know it wouldn't with Little Pete. Especially after they hear you tell them that you saw Carson checking the horseshoes in the barn." I paused. "One thing is certain, he won't be expecting to see us."

"He might go crazy and decide to shoot it out," FW Red added ominously.

I looked down at him and blew softly through pursed lips. "I hope you're wrong. I sincerely hope you're wrong."

We pulled up that evening about a mile or so from the rim. As we squatted around a small fire, I studied the faces of the Comanche warriors I had come to know over the last few days. When I reached Run With Horse, I said, "I must ride on to the ranch alone. There might be trouble. I have to see."

He frowned.

I continued, "A man at the ranch has done many bad things." I gestured to the warriors squatting around the fire. "I do not want any of your men hurt."

Run With Horse grunted and glanced around at his men. Some nodded, for they could follow bits and pieces of our conversation. He pointed to the warriors. "Send one of us. We can slip in with the night as silently as the cougar."

"No." I shook my head and laid my hand on FW

Red's shoulder. "This is our fight. You are our friends. We do not wish you injury."

He studied me a moment, then nodded slowly. "As you wish."

"Place one of your braves on the rim. I will be back in the to signal for you to bring the cattle down the trail."

FW Red interrupted. "But Hobbs, what if—" He hesitated, searching for the right words.

I laughed. "If I don't come back, then you'll know there's trouble."

Chapter Fifteen

The stars illuminated the rolling hills of cedar with a bluish silver light, making finding my way to the trail simple. I was exhausted. Sixteen hours in the saddle, every step jostling my shoulder.

I popped another clove of peyote in my mouth. Over the years, I'd heard white folks belittle Indian medicine, but if their cures were like the one Run With Horse gave me, I'd swear by them. The hole in my shoulder was healing rapidly.

Glancing at the Big Dipper, I guessed the time to be around ten o'clock.

The ranch was about four hours north.

Knowing Runnels believed us to be dead, I napped briefly in the saddle as the wiry little mustang plodded along the shoreline of the Rio Frio. The only plan I had was to slip in and see what I could see. If I got lucky, maybe I could get Coco or O.C. aside.

A quarter of mile from the main house and the outlying buildings, I tied my pony in the middle of a stand of thick cedar.

Fifteen minutes later, I knelt by the corner of the barn. A few frightened nickers came from the horses. I froze, wondering if my clothes had picked up the Indian smell. Then I remembered the grass rope one of the warriors had rigged as a sling for my arm. Hastily, I backtracked beyond the chuck house and hunkered down behind a small cluster of boulders near the trail leading to one of the many pastures on the ranch.

Before I had even settled down, I dozed off, but after a few moments I jerked myself awake. For the next three hours I dozed and jerked awake, dozed and jerked awake. I would have given a month's wages for a good night's sleep.

Abruptly, a pale yellow glow lit the dingy windows of the chuck house. Cookie was up. I didn't want to talk with him. He was old, cantankerous, obstinate, and self-opinionated. Say something was black, he'd insist white. It was as if he took a certain degree of pride in telling you absolutely nothing in such a roundabout manner that you actually thought he was making sense. Then, upon reflection, you realized the old man's words were as empty as a burned-out lantern.

Nope. Cookie was not one with whom I wanted to conspire.

Soon the lights came on in the bunkhouse, and slowly the ranch came to life. I watched from my hiding spot as the wranglers made their way to the chuck house. I resisted confronting Barton when I spotted him. And moments later, Runnels appeared.

I sat back, grinning with satisfaction. They were all here except Carson. That was all right. I'd find him sooner or later.

Backing away slowly, I cut through the trees to my pony.

Had I known the effect of the events to take place within the next two minutes, I would have confronted Runnels and Barton in the chuck house. But I didn't.

The first was Runnels stepping out on the chuck house porch and glimpsing a shadow darting through the trees. The second was just after I mounted, I heard the beat of racing hooves against rock from the south. I pulled up behind a large oak until the rider passed. It was Carson. I could tell from the Montana crown on his John B. He glanced in my direction, but I was deep in the shadows. I didn't figure he even saw me, much less recognized me.

When we rode in that afternoon with the cattle, the ranch was anything but peaceful. The cowhands were hanging about on the porch of the main house.

"What the blazes you figure is going on?" FW Red muttered.

When the hands spotted the Comanches, a shout of alarm sent them scrambling off the porch and into the house. FW Red and I rode forward, holding up our hands and scanning the area for Runnels and his boys. "Don't shoot, Boys. It's me and Hobbs," FW Red shouted.

Tentatively, Coco stuck his head around the door-jamb. "We see you two galoots. What about them Injuns?"

I turned and signaled for Run With Horse to stop the herd. I rode closer to the main house. "They helped FW Red and me bring in the cows. They're friendly."

At that moment, Little Pete burst through the front doorway and raced toward me, screaming, "Lew! Lew! Runnels has done gone and kidnapped Alicia!"

I looked at the house. There stood Miss Louisa and her mother on the porch. Mrs. French was crying and Miss Louisa was comforting her. "When?"

"This morning," he replied, running his words together. "Just after Carson and Runnels spotted you."

"Me?"

"That's what the boys heard."

"That's the gospel, Hobbs," said O.C. "We was in the chuck house when Carson rode up. He'd run that poor horse of his into the ground. I think he might have foundered the animal. Anyway, he told

Runnels he'd spotted FW Red and a passel of Co-manche up on the rim, and them Comanches had the herd that him and Runnels had rustled from Old Pete."

FW Red and I exchanged surprised looks. "Those were his words? That him and Runnels had rustled the cows?"

"Not in so many words, but that's what it amounted to. He told Runnels that the Comanche who had killed Ike Bailey and stolen all hundred head of cows was camped up on the rim." He looked up at me defiantly. "Now you tell me how that jasper could have known about Bailey and the rustling if he didn't have a hand in it."

"That's right," Coco put in. "Then when Carson told him he'd spotted a rider back under the trees, Runnels cussed a blue streak, swearing at Barton and Carson for not making sure FW Red and you were dead."

"And that's when Runnels went crazy," Little Pete said. "He broke in the house and went through Pa's valuables. He took all the money and then he took Alicia."

"How long ago?"

Miss Louisa spoke up, her eyes red. "This morning, about ten." Her eyes grew wide when she spotted my injured shoulder.

"Which way?"

Little Pete pointed toward Camp Verde. "And they was riding hard."

"And Alicia?"

Mrs. French burst into another bout of crying. Miss Louisa's face grew hard. "She went on her own."

I looked at Little Pete. "I thought you said Runnels took her?"

He glared at Miss Louisa. "He did. He took her."

She glared right back at her little brother. "He did not. She went because she wanted to go."

Before Little Pete could respond, Mrs. French ended the conversation. "Your sister is right, Peter John. Alicia went with that man because she wanted to. Now you hush up."

The young boy stared at his mother, his arms stiff at his side, his fists clenched, and tears running down his cheeks. With a shout of despair, he spun and raced for the barn.

"I'm sorry, Ma'am," I said to Mrs. French. "I truly liked your husband. I didn't shoot him."

FW Red spoke up. "He's telling the truth, Ma'am. It was Carson that shot Old Pete. Carson claimed he got the bullet crease on his shoulder when he was running to the house after the first shot. That ain't true. He got it when Hobbs here plugged him."

Her face buried in her handkerchief, Mrs. French didn't reply. Miss Louisa led her back in the house, giving me a wan smile as she passed through the doorway.

I turned to Run With Horse. "Are you hungry? We have food."

His dark eyes swept the ranch. He shook his head slowly. "You and me, and the one with the red hair—we are friends. But the others—they do not trust us, and we do not trust them. We will go."

I offered my hand. "Thank you, my friend."

"And me too," said FW Red, leaning in front of me and sticking out his hand to Run With Horse. "First Comanche I ever got to know. You ain't a bad feller."

From the solemn expression on Run With Horse's face, it was difficult to read just how he felt. He simply nodded and led his men north up the canyon.

"Funny," muttered FW Red. "I got to liking them."

"Me too, but now we got business to tend to." I was worn to a nub, but word of Alicia's flight pumped adrenaline through my veins. "Let's get some fresh animals. Coco, you get us a bag of grub while I get on a shirt that ain't caked with blood."

While I was gingerly slipping into another shirt, Miss Louisa knocked on the bunkhouse door, then peered inside. When she saw I was decent, she came in with a battered Stetson in her hand. "You're riding out?"

I buttoned my shirt. "Yep."

She studied me closely. "For Runnels or Alicia?"

Her question popped me right between the eyes.

I wasn't sure if I'd been avoiding asking myself that question or not. The longer I considered her question, the more I realized I didn't know. Was I using Runnels as an excuse to bring Alicia back? I looked at her. Miss Louisa was a good, decent woman. She deserved the truth.

Before I could reply, her forehead wrinkled and she bit her bottom lip. "You don't have to tell me. Your silence speaks loud enough for you." Tears glittered in her eyes, and she forced a brave smile. "Just be careful. Here." She offered me the hat. "It was Pa's. I saw you lost yours."

I felt like I had done something terrible to her, but all I could do was nod and take the hat.

FW Red stuck his head through the open doorway. "Let's go, Hobbs. We're wasting time."

O.C. and Coco had thrown our saddles on two of the best ponies on the ranch, an iron gray and a roan. Deep-chested and long-legged, they both stood about sixteen hands. They were made for running, and run we did, setting a mile-eating pace when we picked up sign.

"How far you reckon they're ahead of us?" FW Red yelled into the wind.

"Five hours more or less."

"Think they'll camp at Antelope Springs tonight?"

"Dumb move if they do. No, they'll ride through

the night. That's where they have the advantage over us."

"How's that?"

"They know where they're going. We don't. We got to follow their sign. If we ride at night, we could miss their trail if they turned off. Maybe head to Bandera or San Antone."

"Where would you go?"

"San Antone."

We rode until dark, then camped off the trail in the midst of a tumble of boulders. Over a small fire we boiled coffee and gnawed cold beef and biscuits. I leaned back against my saddle, a faint grin on my face.

"What's the grin for?"

I nodded to FW Red's hat. "That looks like Coco's."

He removed the battered brown hat. "It is. I didn't have an extra one, so he gave me his." He shrugged. "Of course, I promised to buy him a new hat if I got someplace to find one."

I removed mine. "Looks like we got a matched pair."

FW Red laughed. "Reckon it does."

Next morning we rode out as soon as we could follow their sign. At times the trail vanished, especially over rocky ground, but between sign in the scattered patches of soil and the scrapes the horseshoes made on rocky plates, we stayed after them, due north.

"Still looks like Camp Verde to me," FW Red said as he leaned from his saddle to study a scar on the face of a limestone plate in the middle of the trail.

He was right. We followed their trail right into Camp Verde.

Just as we rounded the corner of the dry goods store, we came face to face with Joe Carson coming out with a bag in one hand. He dropped the bag and grabbed for his six-gun.

Chapter Sixteen

Instinct took over. Before FW Red could utter a single syllable of warning, fire belched from the muzzle of my Colt.

Carson had not even cleared leather when a patch of blood blossomed in the middle of his chest. He staggered back, his eyes staring at me in surprise. As if in slow motion he brought his left hand to his chest and touched a finger to the spreading circle of crimson.

Smoke drifted upward from the muzzle of my Colt as Carson pulled his fingers away from his chest and stared at them in disbelief. His mouth dropped open. His legs grew rubbery. His eyes rolled up in his head, and he crumpled to the wood boardwalk.

FW Red whistled and looked at me in awe. "Lord

Almighty, that was fast. I ain't never seen nothing like that."

I said nothing. I just stared at the lifeless body on the boardwalk. The bag had fallen open, spilling several cans of beans and peaches on the boardwalk. At that moment, a bald-headed man wearing a white apron and a wizened old man in overalls and a worn straw hat scurried from the general store. They looked down at Carson, then the bald headed man looked up at me. "I saw him go for his first," he said.

"I did too," said the old man, who pointed down the street. "Yonder comes the sheriff."

"Don't worry, Cowboy," said the storeowner. "It was self-defense. I'll swear to that."

I holstered my six-gun and nodded to Carson. "He come in alone?"

"Yep."

The old man in overalls pointed to the end of the street. "He come in from the Bandera road."

"What's going on here?" the sheriff demanded, glancing down at Carson, then eyeing me suspiciously.

The storeowner spoke up. "It was self-defense, Herb. Me and Finas here seen it."

The sheriff continued to eye me. "What's your story, Cowboy?"

"He told you right, Sheriff. Me and my pardner here are after the bunch. They killed Pete French down at the Bar F and stole—"

The sheriff interrupted me. "They did what? Old Pete? They killed him?"

"And stole his savings and kidnapped one of his daughters," aid FW Red. "That's why we're after them."

I glanced at FW Red, but he paid me no mind.

"Poor Old Pete," muttered the sheriff, shaking his head. "He was one of the real old-timers around here. Sure hate to hear that."

I glanced at the storeowner. "Check his pockets to see if he's got enough to bury himself."

The bald-headed man glanced at the sheriff, who nodded for him to take a look.

"About forty dollars," he said, unrolling a wad of bills he had pulled from Carson's pocket.

"That takes care of that. Anything else, Sheriff?"

He waved his hand. "They say it was self-defense, that's good enough for me. You boys get after those varmints. Old Pete was a good man."

Then I remembered the six-gun in my saddlebags with the initials, J.B.A. I pulled it out. "You happen to run across a lawman coming through here sometime back, Sheriff? A ranger. Probably Texas. Maybe Arizona?"

"Why, sure do. Couple weeks back. Knowed him for years. Jimbo Adams. He got word some owl-hoots he'd been hunting for years was down south of here."

I offered him the six-gun. "This his?"

Puzzled, he took the revolver and turned it over

in his hands. "By George, I think it is." He looked up at me. "How'd you come by it?"

Quickly, I explained finding the dead lawman and how I'd later returned to bury him. "The ones who killed him are the same ones who kidnapped Pete French's daughter."

His eyes grew colder. "Then I reckon you best get after them, Cowboy." He held the six-gun up. "You don't mind, I'd be obliged to keep this as a reminder of old Jimbo. We went way back together."

We rode east out of Camp Verde. A dozen unanswered questions tumbled about in my thick head. I pulled my pony down to a walk so I could study the sides of the road. FW Red frowned. "What's wrong? We ain't going to catch up to them like this."

"Sometimes, the smart thing to do is slow down and make sure you know where you're going."

His frown deepened. "I don't follow you."

"Something about this puzzles me. Look at the time. We started out five hours behind them. Even if they made camp last night, they still should have been at least four or five hours ahead when we reached Camp Verde, but Carson was there. Right?"

FW Red pondered the observation. "Okay, so what?"

"It doesn't seem reasonable he would leave the others on the trail and turn back to a town they had passed through earlier just to pick up grub. Why didn't they pick it up when they passed through?"

"Maybe the place wasn't open?"

"Eight o'clock in the morning?" I shook my head. "It was open. They probably rode straight through or around because they didn't want to attract attention, which they would have, especially with a woman riding with them."

He shrugged. "What are you driving at, Hobbs?"

"I think they're out there waiting for Carson to return."

"You mean they're camping out there somewhere?"

I considered his question. "You know, I don't know if they're camping or not."

He frowned. "Now I *am* confused."

I kept my eyes on the sides of the road. "If they were just waiting for him to return with food, why didn't they camp closer to Camp Verde?"

"How do you know they didn't?"

"Explain to me why Carson waited so long to come into town."

"How do you know he waited a long time? You really got me confused now."

"If they rode through about eight this morning and camped fifteen or twenty minutes out of town so Carson could return for grub, he should have picked the supplies up and left by nine, nine-thirty at the latest, not one o'clock in the afternoon."

The light of understanding filled his eyes.

"You're thinking they went to somewhere more permanent a couple hours out."

"That's how I see it. Wherever the place is, it's two hours more or less. Then it takes Carson two hours to return. Four hours altogether, which is just about how far we were behind."

FW Red blew through his lips and reached for his canteen. Holding it in his hand, he gestured to the rough country around us. "Ain't no way we can search all this two hours in every direction."

"No, but we can find a spot and wait until one of them shows up."

A grin ticked up one side of his lips. "Yeah. They're going to wonder about Carson and one of them will ride in to see what's happening."

"And when they do, they'll know we're after them." I glanced over my shoulder. We had ridden about a mile, and I'd seen no evidence of four sets of hooves leaving the road.

"Whoa, Boy." I reined up my pony. I pointed to a rocky hill fifty yards off the road. Thick cedar covered it. "Let's find us a snug spot up there to watch the road."

"What if we're wrong about all this? What if Carson and Runnels had a falling out? For all we know, Runnels and Barton could be close to Bandera now."

"Could be," was all I said, pulling off the road and heading for the hillside. "I sure hope not."

*   *   *

Ten minutes later we were sitting in the shade and gnawing on rock hard biscuits and leather tough jerky. Below us lay the road. We could see for half a mile in either direction.

I flexed my arm. My shoulder stung with each movement, but that was to be expected. I slipped the grass rope from around my neck and let my arm hang down at my side.

"You best not start that thing to bleeding."

"Don't worry, there isn't much of a hole left. That medicine the Comanche spread over it did the job."

He gazed off to the west. "Wonder where them Comanche are about now?"

The afternoon passed slowly. We each napped while the other kept his eyes on the road.

FW Red shook me awake around five or so. Plodding along the road was Frank Barton. "Looks like you were right."

I snugged the pony's cinch. "Get ready. When Barton comes back, he'll be digging the spurs to his horse like Old Beelzebub himself is after him."

Fifteen minutes later Barton raced past.

We fell in behind, trying to round each bend just as Barton rounded the one ahead of us. Worry that we would lose him knotted my stomach.

I guessed he was about fifty or sixty yards ahead of us the last time we spotted him. Then, suddenly, he vanished.

We reined up. "Where the blazes did he go?"

I held my finger to my lips. "Listen."

We grew silent. The only sound was the breathing of our horses and the pounding of our hearts. Suddenly, we heard the sound of snapping branches off to our left. We rode forward slowly, studying the ground.

"Look," whispered FW Red, indicating fresh tracks leading up a narrow trail.

We listened intently, peering into the tangle of cedar and mesquite covering the sloping hill. Another branch snapped. We grinned at each other. Barton!

Leading the way, I turned up the trail. From the animal sign, it was obvious deer and other creatures traveled the trail heavily. I guessed perhaps it led to water, which could be the reason Runnels had selected such an isolated spot. Cover and water. All they needed then was food.

Though steep, the trail was plain. Fresh tracks and horse biscuits marked the way. We paused to listen from time to time, but the sounds from above had vanished.

The trail meandered up the hillside and circled under an overhanging ledge of gray limestone. As we rode from under the ledge, a clattering of rocks sounded from above. I glanced up to see dozens of boulders bouncing down the steep slope, banging into larger boulders and knocking them loose.

"Look out!" I shouted, spurring my gray forward and hoping FW Red could turn back.

One boulder slammed into my horse's right

croup, almost knocking him off his feet, but the frightened animal scrabbled for balance and surged forward, taking us from the path of the landslide.

Several feet up the trail, I reined around.

FW Red was nowhere to be seen. I stood in my stirrups. That was when I spotted his roan under a pile of boulders. I grimaced and hurried back down the trail, a sick feeling in the pit of my stomach.

"FW Red! You hear me?"

A feeble voice edged with pain came from the boulders. "Over here, Hobbs. I'm over here."

I dismounted and picked my way through the boulders. I found FW Red at the edge of the landslide, a large boulder pinning his legs to the ground. He lay flat on the ground, sweat beading his face. Through clenched teeth, he muttered, "I think I'm in bad shape, Hobbs. I can't feel my toes."

I glanced back up the slope. By now Barton must have reached the camp and told Runnels all that had happened. The question now was would they run or come back and pick us off like pesky flies?

I muttered a curse. "Just take it easy, FW Red. I'll get you out of here." Glancing up the trail to make sure no unwelcome company was coming, I led my horse around the jumble of boulders and fastened one end of my rope to the boulder and the other to the saddle horn. FW Red was chewing on his bottom lip, his eyes closed in pain. "I reckon this will hurt," I said.

He grimaced. "It couldn't hurt no worse than right now."

Taking the reins, I tugged at the horse. "Let's go, Boy. Come on. Come on." The large animal strained against the boulder. The rope grew taut, vibrating with tension.

Suddenly the horse lunged forward.

FW Red screamed and fainted.

Chapter Seventeen

The only good part of moving the boulder was that FW Red fainted from the intense pain. I slid him away from the boulders. I felt his legs. I couldn't tell if they were broken or not. I splashed water on his face.

He groaned and shivered.

"Can you hear me, FW Red? Wake up."

Slowly, he opened his eyes. I grinned weakly. "At least you're still alive."

His face was pale. He closed his eyes and licked his lips. "I can't feel my toes, Hobbs. I can't feel my toes."

"What about your legs? Can you move them?"

Though clenched teeth, he muttered, "I'm trying."

His legs didn't budge.

"All right. Take it easy. I'm going to get you on my horse and then back to town. Let the doctor take a look."

He nodded slowly.

I slid my arm under his shoulders. "Now try to sit up."

Clenching his teeth, he struggled upright. I squatted and slipped his arm around my neck and my arm under his. "Here we go." I strained to lift him. He was a dead weight. Slowly, I got him to his feet.

He was shaking his head and tears filled his eyes. "Hobbs, my legs don't move. I can't move my legs."

"Just don't worry about that. The doc will fix them. You just help me get you on my horse." I leaned him against the gray. "Grab the cantle and horn. You pull, I'll lift. Now."

I grabbed him around the hips and lifted him toward the saddle, ignoring his cries of pain. I strained to get one leg high enough to slide his boot in the stirrup. A sharp pain ripped through my shoulder. I grimaced, but continued to shove him in the saddle.

"I'm trying, Hobbs, I'm trying," he said, his words slurred with pain.

Finally I had him in the saddle. I tied his feet in the stirrups and then checked my shoulder. Bright red blood was running down my side. I looked up at him. "Hold tight. I've got to see about your horse."

The roan was dead. I didn't waste time moving

any boulders so I could retrieve FW Red's gear. That could wait. Holding my left hand against the open wound, I picked my way back across the boulders and led my horse down the trail.

Fifteen minutes later, we reached the road. FW Red was clutching the saddle horn with both hands. His head was bowed and his eyes were closed.

"How are you doing?"

He nodded slowly, but the blood seeping from his lips where he had fought against the pain told me he wasn't doing any too well. I had to hurry.

I climbed up behind him, and we headed for Camp Verde. I'd been too busy since the landslide to consider its cause. "Runnels," I muttered. "Just wait."

We had to use the post doctor. After inspecting FW Red, he tended my shoulder by dousing it with alcohol and bandaging it tightly.

The moon had risen by the time he had finished. The doctor looked to be in his mid-forties or so. Slender and serious. "That'll take care of you, Mister Hobbs. Your friend there needs bed rest, and plenty of it."

"What about his legs, Doc? He going to use them again?"

He studied the sleeping man. "Hard to say. The legs are bruised badly. Might be a couple minor fractures, but I couldn't feel them. I'm hoping all the boulder did was pinch some nerves. Now what about you? You have a place to spend the night?"

"I figured I'd be riding out, Doc. I got business to tend to."

He grinned crookedly. "Best business you could tend to tonight, Mister Hobbs, is a good meal, a hot bath, and a good night's sleep. Besides, that wound needs to be cleaned and doctored again in the morning."

The doctor was right. It would be plum pure foolish to go traipsing back up that trail at night. Still, every minute here was another minute Runnels would be ahead of me. I pondered the problem several moments, then shook my head. "Reckon I'll take your advice, Doc."

"Good." At the end of the street is a livery. About halfway down is the Verde Café. Next to it is the hotel and they have facilities for bathing."

I scratched my beard. "Sounds better and better every minute, Doc. Thanks."

Before I went to bed, I checked on FW Red. He was sleeping peacefully. I sure hoped his injuries were not serious.

When I hit the sheets that night, I had clean skin, a full belly, and a tired body. I was asleep before my head hit the pillow.

FW Red was awake next morning when I dropped by.

"I felt my toes this morning, Hobbs. Maybe I'll be all right."

I laid my hand on his shoulder. "You just take care of yourself, you hear? I'll be back to take you to the Bar F as soon as I can."

He nodded. "Be careful."

I didn't know what to expect from Runnels. Would he stand and fight, or run?

Several buzzards lumbered into the air as I approached the landslide. Despite the tumble of boulders on FW Red's horse, I could tell the carrion eaters had been busy overnight. I reined up and dismounted. Rolling a boulder aside, I retrieved FW Red's saddlebags and Winchester. The saddle would have to wait.

I rode slowly and cautiously, six-gun in hand. Birds sang overhead. All seemed normal, and that worried me. I squinted into every shadow, paused at every bend in the trail, and felt my heart skip a beat at every sound.

Several hundred yards beyond the landslide, I glimpsed a cabin through the tangle of mesquite and cedar. I reined up behind a large cedar to study the clearing around the cabin. Smoke rose in a thin column from the chimney, and a single horse stood hipshot in the rude pole corral.

Someone was inside, but who? And where were the other two?

Cautiously, I dismounted, planning to swing wide

around the cabin and come in from the rear. I flexed my fingers about the butt of my six-gun. Silently, I darted through the cedars from tree to tree until I reached the rear corner of the cabin. I pressed up against the logs. My heart thudded in my chest.

Dropping into a crouch, I eased around the corner and slipped along the wall, taking care to duck even lower as I passed under the window. I paused at the next corner, studying the clearing around me, straining to hear any sound that might indicate the return of the two missing horses.

Satisfied no one was within hearing, I eased along the front of the cabin to the door. I figured I'd best hit the floor when I went in, for my eyes would not be accustomed to the dark room. At least on the floor, I wouldn't be as plain a target. I licked my dry lips, looked around once again, took a deep breath, and slammed open the door and leaped inside. I glimpsed a man as I hit the floor and shouted, "Don't move!"

At the same time a woman screamed.

I blinked against the shadows and gaped when I saw Alicia. Standing in front of the fireplace, she was dressed as a man. Her hands, one of which held a wooden spoon, were pressed to her lips, and she was staring at me in shock and surprise.

I jumped to my feet and hastily looked around the room before turning back to her. She was still staring wide-eyed at me. "Miss Alicia? Are you all right?"

The shock on her face faded into disbelief, then glee. She rushed to me, her arms outstretched. "Lew, Lew. It's you. I can't believe it," she cried, throwing her arms around my neck and hugging me. "I've been hoping and praying someone would rescue me from these terrible men. I was terrified of them."

She cried tears of relief into my shoulder, which, coming from a woman who believed I had killed her father, surprised me. Awkwardly, I patted her on the back with my free hand while still clutching my six-gun with the other. "There, there, Miss Alicia. It's all over." At the same time I tried to calm her, Miss Louisa's accusation echoed in my ears. *She went with him on her own.*

From the way Miss Alicia was carrying on, it certainly didn't appear she had accompanied Runnels of her own volition.

She pulled back, wiping at the tears that were cutting streaks in the grime on her cheeks. "I just can't believe it's you." She glanced at the open door. "Where are the others?"

"More important," I replied, "where's Runnels and Barton?" I looked at the pot she had been tending in the fireplace.

"Gone," she said.

"Where?"

She shook her head. "They just left. Took everything and left."

I had the feeling that someone had dumped a puzzle in front of me that was missing one or two pieces, but I didn't have time to worry over it. I grabbed her hand. "Let's go. We don't have anytime to waste."

"Go?" She knit her brows, perplexed.

"Away from here."

"Oh. Oh, yes, yes. I'll get my things," she said.

Quickly I saddled her horse. When I looked around for Miss Alicia she was still in the cabin. "Let's go," I shouted.

Miss Alicia came rushing from the cabin, her hands empty.

I helped her mount. "Where are your things?"

She shook her head. "I decided they were too dirty to bother over. Besides, they might get in our way."

I had more pressing problems on my mind than to question her further. I helped her into the saddle and then swung aboard my own pony. "Stay right behind," I said, heading back down the trail.

At every bend in the meandering trail, I expected to run into Runnels and Barton. I was still puzzled at their disappearance. And I couldn't help wondering why Miss Alicia had not attempted to escape when the two owlhoots had left. On top of that, who was she cooking for? Just her? Would a woman terrified by two men calmly cook herself a meal?

I still had no answer by the time we reached Camp Verde. I put Miss Alicia up at the hotel and stopped by the sheriff's office.

His wife happened to be in the office, and when she heard that Pete French's kidnapped daughter had been rescued, she declared that she would take care of everything. "The poor child must be stricken with fear," she said, marching straight from the office to the hotel.

The sheriff grinned up at me. "You don't got to worry now, Mister Hobbs. Caroline there will see that the young woman is well taken care of."

Then I paid FW Red a visit.

"He's healing good and proper," the post doctor told me before I went in to see my old friend. "He's moving his legs now." He paused and grimaced. "You know, Hobbs, there is a great deal that medicine doesn't know. In another fifty or hundred years, I suppose we might be able to replace about every organ in the body, but now—well, we're still in the Neanderthal days of our profession. I couldn't find any fractures in his legs. There might be some, but they're tiny enough that they should heal without much trouble as long as he takes it easy for the next six weeks or so."

"What about riding? I have a young woman over in the hotel that we need to get back to Frio Canyon. It's about a day-and-a-half ride."

He paused outside FW Red's door and pursed his lips. "Tell him to ride more with his rear than his legs and he should make it with no problems."

I offered him my hand. "Thanks, Doc. I'm much obliged to you."

"When you plan on leaving?"

"As soon as we can."

He nodded, a frown wrinkling his forehead. "Wait until morning. I'd like to keep him here under observation for at least another day."

FW Red grinned like a cat on top of a mouse when I told him I had Miss Alicia and that we were planning on pulling out the next morning.

"Can't be soon enough for me. No, Sireee. What about Miss Alicia? Any trouble?"

I detailed the events of the previous day without revealing the unanswered questions floating about in my head. Their revelation was unnecessary, for FW Red had the same thoughts.

He frowned. "Never can tell about a woman. I figured she'd go at you like wildcat for killing her father."

"Me too. But she didn't mention it." I hesitated, not really wanting to voice my feelings, but at the same time I wanted feedback from FW Red. "You know, I got the feeling she knew I didn't kill Old Pete, but then how would she have learned that?"

His frown deepened. "Something else I don't understand."

"What?"

"You say she was just standing there at the fireplace stirring a pot of stew? She hadn't tried to run from them?"

I nodded. "Yep."

He studied me warily, hesitantly.

"What's on your mind?"

"Well, reckon I was wondering why she was dressed in man's duds and how, if she was so scared, she could stand there and cook. It would make more sense if you'd found her curled up in some corner crying than going about her merry way cooking a meal."

"Well, like I said. When she saw me, she was surprised, and then she started bawling and hugging me about the neck."

FW Red glanced at the ceiling. Finally, in a voice devoid of emotion, he said, "You remember what Miss Louisa and her ma said?"

Reluctantly I grunted. "Yep, but I been trying not to think about that. Miss Alicia sure didn't act like she felt that way to me. Why would she want to make me think anything else?"

His eyes still on the ceiling, he said. "You ever reckoned that maybe she was afraid?"

"Of me? Why?"

"Not you. The law. Maybe she was more involved in what went on at the ranch than we know. Maybe she was afraid that Runnels or Barton might tie her in with the old man's death and the robbery." He shifted his gaze from the ceiling to me. "You see what I mean?"

I blew slowly through my lips. That was one aspect I had not considered. "I'm afraid I do. I am most certainly afraid I do."

Chapter Eighteen

We rode out early next morning, Miss Alicia and FW Red perched on the seat of a Studebaker buckboard the sheriff's wife had insisted the livery owner loan us. She scolded both her husband and the browbeaten livery owner. "It isn't decent for a young woman in a dress to ride a horse."

I rode beside them as we headed southwest. "Might take a few hours longer like this," I said, nodding to FW Red's legs. "But this way you won't take a chance on doing anymore damage to your legs." I glanced over my shoulder. The road behind us was deserted. For some reason, the hair on the back of my neck bristled.

Miss Alicia wore a broad-brimmed hat with flowers and a long-sleeve calico dress against the hot sun. No one spoke much until we took a noon break in the shade of some oaks and pecans along a small stream.

I tended the horses while they sat around the campfire waiting for the coffee to boil. Miss Alicia spread out the lunch the sheriff's wife had prepared. I couldn't help overhearing FW Red say, "That must have been a right scary thing you went through, Miss Alicia."

I peered over the back of one of the horses, watching them.

She nodded emphatically. "It was terrible. I was frightened that they would hurt me."

"Yep. Well, Runnels sure had everyone fooled."

"He certainly did. Why, I was shocked, truly shocked. I knew he was rough, but around me he had always been a gentleman."

"One thing that puzzles me, Ma'am."

She smiled sweetly at him. "Why, whatever is that, FW Red?"

"When they run off and left you, why didn't you get on that horse and try to escape?"

Miss Susanna drew her shoulders together and shivered. With a frown on her face, she replied, "I didn't know where I was, and there were trees all about. I was afraid I would get lost, and then no one would ever find me." Suddenly, her face brightened, and she leaned forward. "Oh, I do think the coffee is ready. Here, hold out your cup." After she filled his cup, she called to me, "Coffee's ready, Lew. Time to eat."

I squatted by the fire, and FW Red and I looked into each other's eyes. From the tiny curl of his lip, I knew he didn't believe a word she said. And I knew for a fact, neither did I.

Mid-afternoon, we paused at Antelope Springs to give the horses a break and pay our respects to Needle, and once again, I looked back over our trail. I had the feeling someone was out there. The remainder of the afternoon was hot and dusty.

Near sundown, FW Red spoke up. "See that yonder line of trees? There's a good spot to camp and plenty graze for the horses."

I arose two or three times during the night, unable to shake the feeling we were being followed, but the night passed uneventfully, and we pulled out bright and early next morning.

The day was another scorcher, hot enough to wither a fencepost. The nagging feeling that someone was behind us bristled the hair on the back of my neck.

"We're getting close," Miss Alicia exclaimed, clapping her hands. "I can't wait to see everyone." She grew somber. "Poor father. I miss him so."

"We all do, Miss Alicia," replied FW Red. He pointed across the prairie. "The road down into the canyon is about a quarter of a mile. From there, it's six miles to the ranch."

A few minutes later, we came in sight of the rim. I looked around at FW Red just as something stung my cheek. A second later, the report of a rifle rolled across the prairie. I slapped my hand to my face and drew back a bloody palm. A bullet had grazed my cheek. If I hadn't turned—

Alicia jumped to her feet in the buckboard and waved her arms frantically. She screamed, "Bart! Help!"

I shucked my six-gun and wheeled my pony about. FW Red already had the buckboard racing to the trail. Everything was moving at breakneck speed. Another shot rang out. A chunk of soil exploded from ground off to my left. I threw a shot in the direction of the bushwhackers and turned to follow the buckboard.

To my surprise, FW Red was trying to fight off Miss Alicia who was struggling to take the reins from him. And then I remembered what she had screamed. Suddenly the missing pieces fell together.

At that moment the buckboard struck a boulder, shattering the left rear wheel and flipping the buckboard. FW Red and Miss Alicia flew through the air. The buckboard skidded to within only a few yards from the rim and the three-hundred-foot drop.

I raced to the overturned buckboard and leaped to the ground just as a slug splatted on the rocks at my feet. My horse bolted. Frantically I dragged FW Red behind the overturned rig, which provided us some protection. I ignored Miss Alicia. Personally, I didn't care if she had busted her neck.

Slugs slammed into the buckboard. They appeared to be coming from the cedars halfway up a nearby hill fifty yards distant. I glanced around for my horse. He had stopped thirty or forty yards away between two cedars. I eyed the Winchester, wishing I had it instead of my Colt, which wasn't accurate much over ten or twenty yards, much less fifty unless a jasper's blessed with enough luck to fill the ocean.

Pain contorted FW Red's face.

I hunkered down at the end of the buckboard and peered toward the hill. "You shot?" I called over my shoulder.

He cursed between clenched teeth. "No, but I sure enough busted my leg this time."

At that moment, another slug tore a chunk out of the buckboard. I jerked back. "Blast! That was close."

They had us pinned down. The nearest cover was a ten-foot cedar a few yards from the end of the buckboard. I wondered if I could reach it and work my way closer to the bushwhackers. I looked around for Alicia. She lay on her stomach several feet from the buckboard.

Straining to speak, FW Red muttered, "You know who them bushwhackers is, don't you, Hobbs?"

I had to chuckle. "I'd be dumber than a grasshopper if I didn't. I had the feeling all along that someone was behind us." I paused and studied the lay of the land. "They can keep us pinned down here as long as they want. I'm going to try to work around them. Get in closer."

Clenching his teeth against the pain, FW Red nodded. "Don't worry about me. I'll be all right." He reached for his handgun and muttered an oath. "I lost my six-gun. It must have fallen out when the buckboard overturned." He looked around. "There," he exclaimed. "There it is. Just this side of Alicia."

I cursed under my breath. Once luck goes sour, it stays sour. "Just stay behind the buckboard, you hear?"

"Yep, I hear."

Rising to a crouch, I waited for the next shot. As soon as it slammed into the buckboard, I broke for the cedar. Several shots rang out, tearing up the ground just behind my heels. I kept waiting for one of those whizzing lead plums to knock me off my feet, but the Good Lord must've been smiling down on me.

When I reached the first cedar, I cut left and dashed behind another cedar, then back to the right behind a third. A cedar won't stop a two-hundred-and-fifty grain slug. All I could do was hope they couldn't figure out which cedar I was hiding behind.

The firing ceased. I paused to catch my breath behind a small cedar. I peered at the hill through the limbs. Maybe they had lost track of me.

I moved cautiously, staying low and avoiding gaps between trees that took more than a couple seconds to cross. The sun beat down. I blinked against the sweat stinging my eyes.

I froze when a feminine voice cut through the hot air. "Lew Hobbs, I have a gun on FW Red. If you don't come out where I can see you, I'll shoot him."

Chapter Nineteen

I remained silent. For all I knew, it could be a ploy for me to reveal my position.

"Hobbs? Did you hear me?"

And maybe she was telling the truth. I decided to risk giving away my hiding spot. "FW Red, you hear me?"

"Yeah, I hear you. She ain't lying. She's got me staring down the muzzle of my own six-gun."

I was playing with a short deck now.

I holstered my Colt and held up my hands as I emerged from the cedar. From the hill came a shout, and moments later, Runnels and Carson were stirring up the dust to get to us.

Miss Alicia eyed me coldly. There was an iciness about her that gave me chills. She motioned me to stand next to FW Red. "Over there. And don't try anything."

Behind me the thundering of the hooves grew closer. I figured FW Red and I were about two minutes from making that last trail drive to the sky.

"Now," Miss Alicia said. "Toss your six-gun on the ground at my feet."

Here was my chance. Just before I reached for it, she cocked the hammer and said, "With your left hand, Mister Hobbs. With your left hand."

By now, the horses were almost upon us.

I eased the Colt out with my left hand as she instructed, and in the same motion of unholstering it, I threw it backhanded at her.

She screamed, dodged, and fired. Behind me a horse squealed. I reached Miss Alicia in one step and ripped the gun from her hand and spun to face Runnels and Barton.

Even as I turned, Barton raced past, yelling at his horse, trying to stop him before the animal went over the rim. Runnels's horse was down, and he was sprawled on the prairie. I didn't know what had taken place, but I leaped for Barton, who fought to control his frightened horse.

From the corner of my eye, I saw Miss Alicia crawling for the six-gun as I grabbed the reins, hoping to throw Barton from the saddle. With a curse, he spurred his horse, frightening it even more. It reared, pawed at the air, then dropped to the ground. Ripping the reins from my hand, it spun and stumbled off the rim, taking a screaming Frank Barton with him.

By now, Runnels was on his feet, charging me like a bull. Staying low, I lunged toward Miss Alicia, who had the six-gun in hand. I grabbed a handful of sand and gravel and tossed it at her just as she fired. She screamed and turned away as I reached her.

Runnels hit us then, barreling us over and sending us sprawling to the ground. I hit, bounced up, and reached him before he could get to his feet. I kicked his six-gun from his hand and then drove a straight right into his forehead.

With a grunt, he leaped to his feet and lunged at me, bellowing like a wild longhorn. I sidestepped and threw a left that split his cheek, but he spun and swung a roundhouse right that caught me on the jaw. Stars exploded in my head.

He waded into me, throwing lefts and rights. I blocked as many as I could, but it was obvious he was stronger. The only way I could take him was by being smarter. Of course, the smart thing would have been never to have gotten in the fight, but I knew that was a moot point when he almost tore one of my ears off.

We stood toe to toe, punching. It felt like I was hitting a tree trunk. When he pulled back for another roundhouse, I grabbed his head and yanked it toward me, at the same time slamming my forehead forward, hard, straight on the bridge of his nose.

Runnels shouted and jumped back, holding both hands to his nose. Blood sluiced through his fingers and dripped from his chin. And then I was all over him like mud on a hog, hitting him with uppercuts, left and right crosses, straight rights, and just about anything else I could find.

His blows lost their steam.

He stumbled forward, and I met him with a right uppercut that rolled his eyes in the back of his head. He stood a moment, and then his legs grew rubbery and he fell to the ground.

I stood gasping for breath.

"Hobbs! Look out! Behind you!"

I spun to see Miss Alicia trying to cock the revolver again. In two steps I reached her and tore the gun from her hand. "I'm keeping it this time," I said, slipping it in my holster.

She hissed at me. "You—why, you—" She leaped at me, trying to tear my eyes out with her nails.

I shoved her away. She stumbled over some rocks and fell to the ground, unhurt except for her feelings. FW Red shouted, "Hobbs!"

When I spun, Runnels had climbed to his feet, holding his six-gun at his side. He grinned wickedly, his teeth red from the blood dripping from his nose. "I'm going to kill you, Hobbs. Then I'll kill that redheaded no-account, and then—"

I cut him off. "Why don't you stop talking and

start doing, Runnels? Or is it just that you're that way with women?"

His face twisted in anger. "Why, you—" He jerked his handgun up.

I didn't even remember drawing. My Colt boomed twice, punching side-by-side holes in his chest just as he leveled the muzzle of his revolver. He got off a shot, but it whizzed harmlessly past. He struggled to get off another shot, but his brain could not get the message to his fingers.

With a long gasp, he sprawled forward on the ground.

When I turned back to Miss Alicia, she lay on the ground, the breast of her pink calico dress stained with blood. She was dead.

Chapter Twenty

After turning the buckboard back over, I tied a sturdy limb to the seat and ran it under the rear axle and several feet beyond. It was a crude skid, but it worked. I loaded FW Red and Miss Alicia in the back and rounded up the horses. I removed Runnels's saddlebags and looked inside. The money appeared to be all there.

And then I spotted the note.

Bart
Hurry. Hobbs is here. He is taking me home.
A.

I frowned as I read the hurriedly scribbled message. When had she written it? Then I remembered the excessive time she had taken in the cabin under the pretense of gathering her garments.

With an angry curse, I crumpled the note.

"What's that?"

Our eyes met. I tossed him the ball of paper. He read it and shook his head. "I never figured that."

I took the note and very deliberately tore it into tiny pieces and threw it to the wind.

FW Red grinned and winked at me.

"Here, hold on to this," I said, handing him the saddlebags.

We headed for Bar F.

"We can send a couple of the boys back to bury this trash," he growled.

As we rode along the shoreline of the Rio Frio, FW Red said, "Since you never wore a gun, Hobbs, I never figured you knew how to use one. But back there, I ain't never seen one that fast."

"I'd just as soon no one knows about that. It's taken me a long time to shake the reputation."

I could feel his eyes on me. I'll give FW Red this, he was no dummy. "Lew Hobbs ain't your real name, is it?"

Giving him a crooked grin, I replied, "Isn't it?"

They carried FW Red in the parlor and set his leg, after which Mrs. French and Miss Louisa attended to Alicia. O.C. and Coco began digging another grave beside Old Pete.

After they had washed and dressed Miss Alicia, they came back into the parlor. "Now, Mister Hobbs," said Mrs. French, her eyes red from crying. "Tell me what happened, please."

I glanced at FW Red and then Miss Louisa. "Well, Ma'am, seems like we were wrong. They kidnapped her. She fought all the way. I thought maybe we were safe when we reached the rim, but I was wrong. After we wrecked, and FW Red busted his leg, me and her stood them off. That's when one of them hit her with his slug." I paused, then added, "She was a true French up to the end, Ma'am."

Tears brimmed Mrs. French's eyes. She leaned forward and laid her hand on mine. "Thank you, Mister Hobbs."

Later, out at the corrals, I was smoking a cigarette and watching the black stallion when Miss Louisa approached me. She had a funny look on her face. Almost mischievous. She leaned her shoulder against a rail and looked up at me. "Well, Lew Hobbs, you are probably one of the most accomplished liars I've ever met."

Surprised, I frowned at her. "Ma'am? I beg your pardon."

"That story you told Ma. You see, I know the truth. I loved my sister, but she never saw things the way we did. When she left, she forgot her diary. Everything's in it. How she planned the robbery with Runnels." She shook her head, biting on her bottom lip to hold back the tears. "I couldn't believe it, but it was there." She sniffed and threw back her shoulders. "I want to thank you for sparing Ma the truth. It would only hurt her."

I nodded, admiring the young woman standing before me.

"What did you do with the diary?"

She turned to watch the black horse. "Burned it."

I thought about the note I had shredded. "So no one else knows, huh?"

Keeping her eyes on the horse, she replied, "Except you. Just like I know your secret."

Suddenly a breath of clean sweet air swept over me. I studied the beautiful valley between the towering rims. "You have a mighty fine place here, Miss Louisa. I'd be much obliged if you'd let me stay on."

She grinned up at me. "Just you try to leave. After all, we have to make sure neither of us tells our secrets." She took a step closer to me. "Don't we?"

I might be dumb, but at least I can track a wagon through a mud puddle. I flipped my cigarette to the ground, put my arms around her slender shoulders and said, "Yes, Ma'am, and I believe I know just how we can carry that out."